Black
Ice

Black Ice

KENNETH J MUNKENS

ISBN 978-0-966-39512-9

Printed in the U.S.A.

For
John Dwight Munkens,
my father,
who gave me the strength
to move invisible mountains.
You are missed.

CHAPTER 1

"This can't be happening," Shaun thought as his car slid on black ice toward the back of an eighteen wheeler that was stopped at a traffic light. It seemed to happen in slow motion. Yet, the impact was jarring. His seatbelt kept him from flying forward and he never saw the airbag deploy. An awful sound of plastic and metal being bent, twisted, and broken told him his new car wasn't new anymore. Funny how, at times like these, one's brain analyzes and addresses so many different factors at the same time. His car was damaged—maybe totaled, he was alive and relatively unhurt even though there was pain in his right arm, his insurance rates were sure to go up, the client waiting for the blueprints he was carrying was going to be pissed, the next hour promised to be a frustrating mess, Alicia was going to say, "You need to be more careful," it's cold out there and he's not dressed appropriately, and . . .

A knock on his window got his mind to focus.

"Buddy, are you alright?" A six-foot-tall, slender, man in his thirties wearing a brown leather bomber jacket and "Indiana Jones" fedora asked.

"Uh, Yeah . . . I think so," Shaun replied through the glass.

"Well, your car's not," the man stated the obvious. "I alerted the police and better get these flares out before we start piling up cars like cordwood."

Shaun unlocked his seatbelt and tried to open the door but it was stuck. When he shoved against it, it refused to give. He looked at the wreckage of his new Chevrolet Camaro. For a low speed crash it was really torn up. "I bet the frame is bent," he said to himself. "Damn it!"

The man he had talked with returned. "We better exchange information," he suggested.

"The door is jammed. I'll have to get out the other side."

"Be careful, it's icy."

Like I don't know that, Shaun thought as he climbed over the console to get to the other door. Unfortunately, he found that door wouldn't open, as well. After turning the key to accessories he was able to run the window down and climb out of the automobile.

"I think you bent my license plate," the truck driver stated.

"You trying to be funny?" Shaun snapped.

"Just trying to lighten up the situation," he replied.

"There's no lightening up the situation. The situation sucks!"

"You're bleeding," the Indiana Jones lookalike pointed out.

Shaun looked at his right arm and blood stains had formed on his white shirt.

"Probably the airbag," the other driver surmised, "They designed the silly things so that when they deploy the plastic cover flies at you like shrapnel from a claymore."

"This is just not how this day was supposed to go," Shaun mumbled as he retrieved the information needed to exchange with the driver of the brick wall. What he didn't know, at that moment, was that this day was not going to go the way he could have ever imagined.

Over the next forty-five minutes a police cruiser arrived, an accident report was written, the mangled car was pulled up onto a flatbed tow truck, Shaun put on his suit jacket but still shivered in the cold, and he learned the name of the truck driver was Indiana Jones. The driver explained that his parents were big fans of the film, *Raiders of the Lost Ark*. He went on to complain, "With a name like that you have to dress like this. I wanted to be a ballet dancer." Shaun didn't react to the obvious humor. Instead he stood on the curb holding blueprints and tried to locate a taxi service on his smart phone.

"Where do you need to go?" Indiana asked.

"Ballantine Business Center downtown but I'll never make it on time. I'm screwed!"

"Get in. I'll take you there."

"Thanks, but I better wait for a taxi."

"You'll freeze waiting for a cab if you could even get one to come out in weather like this. Get in, it'll be quicker. I don't bite. Unless you're a chick and we're . . . well, anyway, I don't bite."

Reluctantly, Shaun climbed up into the cab of the blue Kenworth T700 truck. The inside was warm and comfortable.

The truck driver climbed in and said "Buckle up the roads are slick."

Shaun didn't laugh but began to ask, "Indiana . . . "

The curtain to the sleeping quarters of the big truck opened and a twelve-year-old girl poked her head out and said, "What are you doing crashing into our home?"

Indiana said as he began driving the truck, "Sweetie, this is Shaun Harper. Shaun this is my daughter Kimberly. We are currently between residences at the moment. Therefore, this is our home." He blew the air-horn twice to punctuate his statement.

Shaun looked at the twelve-year-old girl. She had auburn hair pulled back into a ponytail, wore an orange sweatshirt with the Texas longhorn on it, and black sweat pants. "I really didn't do it on purpose," he stated.

"I know—it's slippery out there."

"I'm aware of that." Shaun thought for a moment and then asked, "If you don't have an address what did you give the police?"

"The same address that's on my license. It's a bit dated."

The big rig moved slowly down the road as Indiana went through the gears and watched the road for other patches of ice.

"What's that?" Kimberly asked pointing at the blueprints.

"What? Oh, these are plans for a new building my company is . . . was going to build."

"Is that what you do—build buildings? That's so cool."

"Well, these plans and cost estimates have to be delivered by nine to be considered."

"I'm working on it," Indiana chimed in.

"How do you live in a truck?" Shaun asked impulsively.

"It's fun. I have the upper and dad the lower. We're on tour."

"Yeah, we're going all over this big beautiful country," Indiana said enthusiastically.

"I want to see and touch and smell and taste and hear everything," Kimberly said with an obvious sense of anticipation. "But, first I need a shower. Dad we have to find a place to get a shower."

"I'll see what I can do."

Shaun commented, "You have to find places to shower?"

"It's not hard, the Y, health clubs, churches, car washes . . ."

"Only in the summer," Kimberly added.

"Listen, you can use the shower at my house," Shaun heard himself say while wondering why. At the time he had no way of knowing that it would be a life-changing invitation.

"You're on," Kimberly said.

"There, up ahead, some more black ice," Indiana pointed out.

"How can you tell?" asked Shaun.

"No road is completely flat. They all have a grain. When it looks smooth something is causing it—that something is ice."

They arrived at the Ballantine Business Center at five minutes before nine. Shaun grabbed his blueprints and said, "I appreciate you getting me here." He looked at Kimberly and remembered his offer so added, "You have my address. I will be home in a few hours."

"We'll wait for you. Give you a ride home," Indiana replied.

As he entered the building Shaun looked out at the eighteen wheeler parked in the far end of the parking lot and wondered what Alicia was going to say.

CHAPTER 2

"You need to be more careful," Alicia, Shaun's wife, warned.

"It was black ice," Shaun protested, "You can't see black ice." After a pause, he corrected himself, "Of course, if the road looks smooth—there's ice."

Alicia asked, "Well, where are they—your new best friends."

"They're getting a change of clothes, so that they can each take a shower." He looked out the window of their 3,000 square foot brick colonial home at the eighteen wheeler parked in front. He figured that the father and daughter were probably living in thirty square feet. Also, he knew a big rig parked on the street would definitely get their upscale snooty neighbors talking. Any time anything disrupts the pastoral, pristine splendor of their exclusive neighborhood the tongues start wagging, fingers pointing, and Home Owners Association gestapo marching. He expected a call before the day was over.

"I guess they might as well stay for dinner," Shaun heard Alicia say behind him. Her voice was more welcoming and hospitable.

Indiana and his daughter Kimberly each had a much welcomed and extended shower. After some arm-twisting they were convinced to stay for dinner. At first, Indiana wanted to get back on the road, but when Kimberly was tempted with spaghetti he relented.

At dinner Alicia commented on the violin case that Kimberly had brought in with her. The twelve-year-old beamed that it was a custom handmade violin made by a world renowned luthier in North Carolina. She went on to explain that hers was a Guarneri-style violin inspired by Giuseppe Guarnerius del Gesu, an 18th century Italian craftsman.

"The Guarneri-style has a larger body than a Stradivari," Kimberly explained, "This gives it greater air volume and stronger wood vibration. It's louder and I believe more capable of a wide range of emotion."

"Would you play for us after dinner?" Alicia asked.

"You mean play for my dinner?" Kimberly replied with a stern look on her face. The room fell silent. Then Kimberly smiled a twelve-year-old smile and added, "I'd be delighted."

They settled in the den and prepared to hear a few simple tunes from her lesson book. Kimberly stood before her audience and tuned the violin. She then closed her eyes and began with Ludwig van Beethoven's *Violin Concerto in D major, Op. 61.* Pure dulcet tones and waves of emotion filled the room. Caught totally by surprise both Shaun and Alicia knew this wasn't any child playing children's tunes. It was a talented, well-trained professional who played for her dinner.

The next piece was the *Violin Concerto in D major, Op. 35,* written by Pyotr Ilyich Tchaikovsky. It is considered to be one of the most technically difficult works for violin. Flawlessly performed, the home of Shaun and Alicia Harper became a concert hall. Beautiful tones and the emotions they stirred brought tears to Alicia's eyes. Shaun was amazed that Kimberly played these entire concertos without music. Eyes closed, she played the instrument lost in a world of her own. Little did Shaun and Alicia know that they would soon enter that enigmatic world.

After an hour Indiana thanked their hosts for the shower and dinner. It was time to get back on the road. However, Shaun and Alicia were not ready to let go. They invited their two guests to remain the night.

"We have plenty of room and would love to have you stay," Alicia offered.

"You've been kind enough," Indiana said, "Besides, we have to continue the tour."

The telephone rang and Shaun answered it. After a few minutes he returned and explained, "That was the head of the HOA. They wanted to know if we were moving. When I told them no, they wanted to know how long the 'big truck' was going to be parked in front of our house."

"That didn't take long," Alicia commented sarcastically.

"See, its better we get our 'big truck' out of here," Indiana stated.

"No, the 'big truck' isn't the problem," Shaun declared, "The big noses of busybodies are the problem. We'd like the two of you to stay. Please."

Indiana looked at his daughter who had remained standing silently during the exchange. No words were spoken yet they communicated. Slowly, Kimberly placed her violin into its case and shut it.

"I think its best that we leave," Indiana concluded, "There's a lot to be done."

Alicia intervened, "The roads are icy . . ."

"Black ice . . ." Shaun interjected. Indiana smiled.

Alicia continued, "After a good night's sleep and pancake breakfast, your journey will be so much safer."

Once more father and daughter exchanged glances. Then Kimberly said, "Do I have to play for my breakfast, as well?"

"No," Alicia answered.

"Oh, then my playing tonight wasn't adequate?"

"No," a confused Alicia said, "I mean yes, it was beautiful. More than enough payment for dinner. We were so impressed at how well you play. Thank you."

"She's toying with you," Indiana explained.

"I see," Alicia glanced at Kimberly who simply smiled.

With their bedrooms prepared, Kimberly excused herself and the adults settled in the den.

"She plays beautifully," Alicia concluded, "You must be very proud."

"A combination of practice, desire, and talent," Indiana stated in an uncharacteristically cool voice. His demeanor was that of someone who had a compelling story, but one that was not going to be told. With this dismissive answer Indiana made it clear that the subject was closed.

"What's your next stop on the tour?" Shaun changed the subject.

"We're headed south following the geese."

"Is there a destination?" Alicia asked.

Indiana looked at Alicia and seemed lost in thought. "An interesting thing about destinations. They force one to follow a certain path. We don't do that. Sometimes they create timing issues which can lead to stress and other problems," he glanced at Shaun. "Kim and I are on the 'spit in eye' tour. The next stop will be when we stop. No timetables. No destinations. Tonight, this was our destination. Unplanned, greatly appreciated, tomorrow we continue on the next leg."

"Spit in whose eye?" Shaun inquired.

"God's."

From upstairs they heard a distant violin. Kimberly was going through her scales perfecting the tone of each note.

An uneasy silence hung in the den until Alicia asked, "Doesn't Kimberly go to school?"

"She's truck schooled," Indiana offered, "We are doing fine. Please, don't be concerned about us."

The rest of the evening was less of a cross examination

with pleasant conversation. Throughout the evening Kimberly played in her room. They heard Ralph Vaughan Williams' *Lark Ascending,* Bruckner's *Symphony No. 4 in E flat major* known as the *Romantic Symphony,* numerous concertos, and parts of symphonies.

When Shaun and Alicia were finally in bed they expressed their concerns.

"It's unnatural to practice that long," Alicia stated.

"Well, she plays beautifully and probably loves doing so," Shaun commented.

"Is it her desire or her father driving her?" Alicia wondered.

"It's none of our business."

"It is, if the welfare of a child is at stake."

"Don't get involved."

Alicia had already decided to get involved. If she felt Kimberly was being unreasonably forced to practice by her father to fulfill his dreams and expectations she would put a stop to it. The child deserved a childhood. However, the next day would not bring what Alicia expected.

Shaun and Alicia fell asleep to the distant sound of a violin.

CHAPTER 3

Shaun and Alicia awoke to the distant sound of a violin.

"Did she ever sleep?" Alicia asked her husband.

"I don't know. I did."

"I'm really concerned about the poor child."

"I still say that it's none of our business."

"It is! We can't ignore what appears to be a form of abuse."

At breakfast Alicia attempted to get a better perspective on Kimberly's violin playing and practicing. She told the twelve-year-old how beautifully she played and how it must take a great deal of practice. When Alicia asked how much she practices Kimberly glanced at her father, who was watching the exchange, and said that she had to practice as much she can. This made Alicia more suspicious about what was taking place.

"Time for us to hit the road," Indiana announced. "Thank you for the showers, meals, and comfortable beds."

Kimberly went upstairs to retrieve her clothes and violin.

"Mr. Jones," Alicia began, "I'd like a word with you."

"Pick your word," he replied with a smile.

"It may not be my business, but I'm concerned about Kimberly."

"You don't need to be concerned. She's healthy, happy, and gets a hot shower from time to time. It's all part of being on tour."

"Spit in eye tour," Shaun added.

"Right."

"Don't you think that you are pushing her too hard?" Alicia asked.

"There is no pushing at all."

"All the practicing, dragging her around the country, no home life, no education, it's not good for a young girl to live that way."

Indiana sat silently for a moment. He picked up a spoon and stirred the remains of his coffee. By all appearances he was considering saying something, yet was not ready to do so. He lifted the spoon out of the cup and placed it in the saucer. He looked up and said in a controlled voice, "We appreciate your hospitality and kindness. Now, we have to move on. Let's leave it at that."

"I can't," Alicia insisted, "I don't want to interfere. Please understand, I only want to help you and Kimberly."

"We are not in need of any help," Indiana stated. "We . . ."

Violin music drifted down from an upstairs bedroom. Kimberly played *Pavane for a Dead Princess* by French composer Maurice Ravel. It was written in 1899 for solo piano. The composer published an orchestrated version in 1910. The three adults in the kitchen fell silent. The piece was Indiana Jones' favorite and was a young girl with a violin's way of saying I love you. Her father sat listening to slow, tender, haunting sounds reaching out to him, reassuring him, and telling him that they were doing the right thing. He swallowed and held back tears for the ten-millionth time.

When the piece ended, Indiana Jones rose from the table and said, "We have to leave." He added with a lighter tone, "Besides, I have to get that big truck out of your neighborhood."

"Don't!" Alicia said abruptly.

"What is it that you want?"

"I need to know that you are not stealing her childhood in pursuit of some misguided fame and fortune. Let her have a childhood."

"She's not living a childhood. She's living her life," Indiana stated firmly.

"If you leave, I'll call child services and put in a complaint."

"You do what you have to," the truck driver said as he turned to leave the kitchen, "We'll be out of the state in a few hours."

"You gave the police false information," Shaun interjected. Indiana turned to face Shaun, who added, "Your license has the wrong address. For all I know it is invalid. One call and the big truck isn't going anywhere."

"The price of a meal keeps going up," Indiana stated as he returned to the table. "I could be angry with you for interfering where you don't belong. You do, however, think you are doing the right thing—no matter how wrong you are."

From the bedroom came more violin music. Beautiful emotional tones strung together in a manner that reached into the hearts of all three adults. It was unfamiliar music, yet spoke of meadows and streams and sunlight and life.

In a whisper Indiana said, "She's thinking." This time a single tear escaped from his eye. The expression on his face caused both Alicia and Shaun to sit in silence and wonder if what they were trying to do was indeed wrong. A father's love cannot be hidden. A father's pain is forever.

Indiana looked at the couple sitting at the table and explained, "When Kim is in a pensive mood she plays from the heart. It's her expression. Never the same. Never recorded. And, I never stop her."

"That's her music?" Alicia asked.

"Those are her thoughts."

"She loves music?"

"She is music."

"Then, it's not you driving her."

"It's me driving her," he said in a lighter tone, "around the country." Then in a more serious tone he said, "Kimberly is a remarkable young lady. You can hear her talent. I don't have to push her. She has an obsession born of life's events. I will support her and take her to the ends of the earth if it allows her music to continue."

"Why are you traveling around the country?" Shaun asked. "With her talent she could play in any orchestra or be a soloist."

"That's not what she wants."

"What does she want?" Alicia asked as she continued to listen to the soft, rich, full-toned music that escaped from a young girl's heart.

"She wants to continue the tour."

"Why spit in God's eye for such a wonderful talent?" Shaun asked.

"Just like there was a price to pay for two meals, there is a price meted out for talent."

"Please," Alicia said softly, "help us understand."

Indiana rose from the table. He walked over the kitchen window and looked out. It was an overcast day—grey and foreboding. The roads would be treacherous. He thought of all the weeks they had been on tour and all the places where they stopped. Kimberly played at churches, in restaurants, in parks, on stages from time to time, at schools, and any other place where she wished to leave her indelible mark of music. No childhood? Maybe. But theirs' would be a great adventure that eclipsed even the best childhood. Kim deserved—no earned—no less. Indiana decided the price he had to pay for he and Kim to get back on tour would be the telling of their story to two strangers who gave them a meal.

The music stopped.

CHAPTER 4

Kimberly entered the room carrying her violin case and backpack. She walked over to her father and hugged him, then said, "I packed your bag, but remember to brush your teeth."

Indiana put his arm around his daughter and told her of the Harper's concerns about her welfare. He left out the threats. She listened. When her father told her that he was considering telling their story she nodded. Slowly, Kimberly walked over to the door that led into the living room stopped and said, "I don't wish to be here. Where are the keys?"

"In my jacket pocket," Indiana replied.

Kimberly left the room, retrieved the keys, and went out to the blue Kenworth. After a few minutes they heard the truck engine start.

"Should she be out there doing that?" Shaun asked with concern.

"She knows how to start the engine," Indiana answered, "She also knows how to drive the truck."

"She's not going to drive it now?" a near panicked Shaun asked.

"No, she needs the engine running for the heat to work. It's cold out there."

"I hope we didn't upset her," Alicia commented.

Indiana looked at Alicia for a prolonged period. He then looked out the window at the parked truck and began, "When Kimberly was five years old she could read at the middle school level. Her mother and I knew she was smart. After all, she was our kid and every parent thinks their child is exceptional. In this case she was." He turned to face Alicia and Shaun, "At five she expressed an interest in music so we bought her a keyboard. You wouldn't believe how quickly she was able to play complex tunes. Her attention then turned to the violin. Of course, we had to get a student violin because her hands were too small for a full size one. She took lessons and progressed at a rapid pace. We went through violin teachers like you do shoes as a kid grows."

Outside they heard the truck's air-horn blast twice. Indiana smiled, "Good morning Home Owners!"

"The telephone should ring any minute," Shaun observed.

The telephone rang.

After a conversation Shaun returned to the kitchen and announced, "The head of the HOA told me what time it was. She also asked when the big truck was leaving."

"What did you tell Bridgett?" Alicia asked.

"I asked, is it still there?"

Indiana chuckled. "I'd better finish our story so that we can get the big truck out of here."

"Oh, no, stay till the weekend," Shaun replied.

Indiana picked up the story, "Kimberly didn't do well in school. They couldn't figure out what to do with her. She couldn't sit in kindergarten while reading Moby Dick. Yet, there were some things that she needed to be taught, like social skills, so we tried to keep her in the school system. That didn't work. Older kids, who she outperformed, picked on her and made fun of her. She was smart but emotionally she was a child who didn't understand what she did wrong. Finally, we decided on home schooling. She passed all of the tests to graduate high school at the age of nine."

Shaun and Alicia looked at each other feeling rather foolish about expressing concerns about Kimberly not going to school. Alicia walked over to the window next to Indiana and looked out at the blue truck. Inside the cab was a gifted child—a child who played music more beautifully than she had ever heard. She was also a highly intelligent child. Shaun's wife couldn't help but wonder if traipsing around the country in a big rig wasn't a waste of Kimberly's talent and her potential.

"Mr. Jones," Alicia asked, "do you think dragging Kimberly around the country with no roots and few opportunities is the best thing for the child?"

Indiana turned to look at Alicia. The expression on his face didn't reveal anger or frustration as one would expect. Rather, his countenance was that of someone who knew the facts and, as a result, saw the foolishness of her question.

"Just after Kimberly received her high school diploma she started having pain in her lower back. The doctors discovered a rare form of cancer. I can't tell you the name. I call it the Terrorist Cancer because they explained that it is unpredictable and can strike anywhere in the body. It was slow growing but depending on where it attacked could be fatal. They talked us into surgery." He looked out the window, "Kim was brave and came through the procedure well. She has always had a sense of humor. Maybe others don't always understand but she can play you just like she plays her violin."

"I know," Shaun commented.

Indiana walked over to the door that led to the living room. He examined the room or searched for the correct words. The Harper home was well furnished and reflected wealth. It struck him as strange that he should be standing here when they needed to get back on the tour. He turned around. "Medical bills started pouring in. It's like dealing with the I.R.S. when it comes to insurance companies. They have clauses and conditions and requirements and smoke and mirrors that rationalize why they will pay far less than expected. An anesthesiologist replaced one who had become ill and the insurance company explanation of benefits had footnote P165 'non-approved professional' which rejected the charge." Indiana scratched his head. "I'm just a truck driver. I had to take more and longer routes to earn more money. This kept me away from home for two or three nights a week. My wife had to handle the doctor visits, home schooling, violin lessons, and the house. It wasn't easy."

"When Kim was ten-years-old the doctors discovered something that concerned them. How they even found it I have no idea. There was a small growth on the optic nerve of her right eye. Because of its location they couldn't do anything—not even a biopsy. All they could do was watch it." Indiana paused. A father's fear and concern for his child was evident.

Shaun and Alicia sat in silence. What began as a magical story of a remarkable life was becoming a human tragedy. They had opened the door and now were destined to step through it. Both were unaware of how it would all turn out or that they would play a pivotal role.

Indiana continued, "Since then the growth has increased in size and another has appeared on her left optic nerve."

"What do the doctors say is the prognosis?" Alicia asked in a soft concerned voice.

"While they can't be sure, based on the progress of the disease, Kimberly will be blind by the time she reaches sixteen." Even the strongest face cannot hide sorrow that reaches into one's very soul.

"Isn't there anything that they suggest could be done?" Shaun asked. In the back of his mind he thought how ridiculous he had been worrying about a wrecked car.

Indiana shook his head and shrugged, "Nothing."

"She knows this is going to happen?" Alicia asked.

"That's why we are on tour. Kimberly wants to see and feel as much of America as she can—while she can. And, by god, I'm going to help her." Once again, Indiana paused. "She told me that she wanted to fill her head with visual memories."

"How is she handling it?" Alicia asked.

"Kimberly is a remarkable young lady—more remarkable than you realize. I don't know how she is handling it or how she handled what followed. She has a strength inside of her that makes me feel like a coward." Indiana looked out the window. "I was 642 miles away when I got the call."

CHAPTER 5

Indiana walked over to the kitchen table and sat down. Instinctively, Alicia got the coffee pot and filled their guest's cup. After stirring the liquid and gaining his composure Indiana continued the tale of a father and daughter on tour, "Kimberly's mother carried so much of the burden with doctors, schooling, music, bills, and a daughter facing an uncertain future. Me, I was always on the road earning money. I called every day and we all spoke, but I wasn't physically there to help. In truth, I'm not sure that I was emotionally there either."

"You were doing what you had to do to support your family," Shaun offered.

"Kimberly's mother was the strength of our family. She kept everything going. I wasn't there to see the toll it was taking. When you look back you ask yourself, 'why didn't I see that,' but the simple answer is you weren't looking for it. I was 642 miles away when I got the call."

Silence filled the kitchen as both Shaun and Alicia didn't want to interrupt and Indiana Jones sought the strength to continue.

After what seemed a protracted length of time Indiana continued, "Kimberly called me." He stirred his coffee with a spoon in his right hand which trembled. "I was on a highway doing sixty." Another pause. "Kimberly . . . told me . . . that she found her mother . . . dead in the basement." As he relived the moment he found that he couldn't continue speaking. Slowly he lifted his coffee cup and took a small sip. With shaking hands he placed the cup back in the saucer. "She had gotten out of bed in the morning and couldn't find her mother. Thinking that she had gone to the store, Kimberly played her violin. When her mother hadn't returned after an hour, Kimberly looked for her." Indiana rose from the table and walked over to the window. He looked out at the blue cab of the tractor trailer. Inside he could see shadows of movement. Kimberly was playing her violin. "I was 642 miles away when my daughter told me she found her mother hanging in the basement."

Alicia gasped.

"The poor child," Shaun whispered.

Indiana turned around. He looked at the couple and said, "Do you want to know the meaning of helpless? It's being twelve hours away when your daughter needs you most."

"I'm so sorry," Alicia said as tears flowed from her eyes.

"An eleven-year-old shouldn't ever have to have that kind of experience," Indiana said, "I had her call the police and told her I would get home as fast as possible." The shaken truck driver paced around the kitchen. He finally stopped in front of the window once more. As he looked out he said, "Kimberly went through a long period of mourning. She had to ride with me on my runs because I couldn't leave her home alone. It turned out to be the best thing for both of us."

Shaun and Alicia looked at each other unable to think of anything to say that might be helpful.

After getting through the most difficult part of the story, Indiana seemed slightly more relaxed. He returned to the table and sat. "In the beginning Kimberly was quiet. Frighteningly quiet. Just getting a yes or no was all that I could hope for. Then one day she was sitting in the passenger seat watching the road and said, 'I don't want to go home.'"

"I understand her not wanting to face the memories," Alicia said.

"That's what I thought, but Kimberly is a unique beautiful young lady," Indiana answered, "When we stopped we discussed her feelings and reasons for not wanting to go home." For the first time there was a hint of a smile on Indiana's face. He continued, "Kimberly told me how much she missed her mother and how much she loved her. Then she said, 'I can only express my love with that which I love—music.' She opened her violin case, took out her violin, and played a short symphony that celebrated her mother's life. It had upbeat parts and very solemn sad parts. Throughout there was a recurring theme that she later said was the joy of a daughter whose life was touched by a loving mother. She found her way to cope." He looked directly into the cup of coffee and revealed, "I only wish I had found a way."

The telephone rang and Alicia answered it. After a moment she handed the receiver to Shaun and said, "It's for you."

Shaun spoke on the telephone for a few minutes then hung up. He returned to the kitchen and told Alicia, "We got the convention center project."

"That's wonderful," Alicia exclaimed, then caught herself.

"Is that the job you had to deliver the plans for yesterday?" Indiana asked.

"Yes. It's a big project and will be very . . . profitable," Shaun's voice trailed off as he thought about all they had just heard about a little girl handling life's terrible hard knocks. Somehow the good news felt out-of-place or, at the very least, poorly timed.

"That's great," Indiana said with enthusiasm and a brighter countenance. "I guess we better get the big truck out of here to let you folks get back to your lives."

"Please, finish your story," Alicia asked, "Why didn't

Kimberly want to go home?"

"I wish I could explain it as well as Kimberly did. She first told me that her mother wasn't at home but was in her heart and her music. So, no matter where we went her mother was with her. Then she said she wanted to be with me." Indiana shrugged as if wondering what he could offer such an amazing child. "She said we needed each other. We needed to help each other get past these tough days. She said she didn't want to go home because that would be going back and we needed to follow a new path." Indiana looked at Alicia and Shaun, then added, "I asked Kimberly what she wanted, what would be something that would make her happy once more. She stayed quiet for a long time. Then she jumped up and said, 'I'll get back to you on that.' We had stopped in a rest area and planned to spend the night. Kimberly walked over to a picnic table and began playing her violin. It seemed so out of place yet so perfect. She was thinking. Before long people who had stopped at the rest area began to sit at other tables and listen to Kimberly. Quite a crowd gathered. So much so, that the highway patrol came by to investigate." For the first time Indiana smiled, "You know those two police officers hung around and listened until they received a call about an accident. As people left to continue their journeys many placed money on the table next to Kimberly. She made over a hundred dollars that night and the tour was born."

"So, you go around playing for tips?" Shaun asked.

"You missed the point," Indiana stated, "We are going around America seeing everything that we can see. Kimberly answered my question that night as to what would make her happy. She told me that she wanted to have as many pictures in her mind as possible when the darkness comes. And that, my friend, is what I am going to give her—as many sights as is humanly possible." Once more Indiana stood and walked over to the window and looked out at the big truck parked in front of the house. He continued, "I sold the house and bought a 40 foot trailer. I already owned the Kenworth T700. We packed what belongings and furniture we wanted to save in the back, fueled up, and hit the road."

"Isn't there anything that can be done to save her eyesight?" Shaun asked.

"According to half a dozen doctors there is nothing that can be done."

"It just seems so unfair," Alicia commented.

"It is unfair," Indiana agreed, "That's why it's the 'spit in eye' tour."

"God's eye," Shaun said.

"Darn right."

The front door opened and Kimberly entered the house. She walked into the kitchen and asked her father, "Have you finished our tale of woe?"

"Sure have sweetie."

"Then we need to get back on tour."

"I need to brush my teeth. Wait here. I'll be right down." Indiana left the kitchen.

Shaun, Alicia, and Kimberly remained in the kitchen in awkward silence.

"Beethoven became deaf," Kimberly said, "At the premiere of his *Ninth Symphony* he had to be turned around to see the audience applaud because he couldn't hear them. Even in the dark I'll be able to hear the music and feel its emotion. Guess I shouldn't complain."

"You are a very brave young lady," Shaun acknowledged.

"When you choose to face something it's bravery, when you accept something that is inevitable it's resolve."

"It still takes courage," Alicia added.

"I'm not brave and I wish things were different, but they're not. Every day that I see the light, I want to use that light to see whatever presents itself. Maybe Beethoven wrote music as fast as he could when he knew his hearing was going. I'm learning music as fast as I can so that I can play in the dark."

Indiana returned to the kitchen with his bag and wearing his hat and coat. "Let the tour continue," he announced.

Kimberly ran over to her father and hugged him. She stated, "I warmed up the truck for you."

Shaun walked over to Indiana and offered his hand, "Thank you for being so patient with us. We meant only the best. We won't soon forget the two of you. Send us some postcards from the tour."

"Spit in eye tour," Kimberly added.

"Yes."

Father and daughter turned to leave.

"Wait!" Alicia called. It was then that she surprised the other three in the room.

CHAPTER 6

Indiana, Kimberly, and Shaun stared at Alicia waiting to hear her next words. The five foot six, middle-aged, blond stood before them wearing a blue bathrobe and fuzzy slippers. She attempted to pour a cup of coffee but found the carafe was empty. After a few moments, she spoke while choosing her words carefully, "I don't want you to leave." There was a pause then she added, "Yet. It's important that we talk, first."

"We appreciate your hospitality but we really need to get going," Indiana stated.

"I want you to go," Alicia replied nodding her head.

"So, it's settled," Shaun added quickly.

"No, it's not," Kimberly observed as she walked over to Alicia and asked, "What's wrong?"

Alicia found herself unable to answer. Tears ran down her face. She looked at Kimberly, then Indiana, and finally Shaun. Silence filled the kitchen. She reached out and took Kimberly's hands. Alicia finally spoke to Kimberly, "I know us coming together was an accident—literally. But, sometimes they're not accidents."

"Trust me it was an accident," Shaun interjected.

Alicia turned her attention to Shaun and countered, "Sometimes its fate, kismet, call it what you will." She returned to Kimberly, "Deep inside I feel there is a reason we came together. It's something we shouldn't ignore. If we let this opportunity slip away we may live to regret it."

Kimberly looked around the kitchen. It was neat and clean, except for the breakfast dishes. In fact, the entire house was orderly and immaculate. It had style but lacked substance. While not an unhappy home it was devoid of emotion. Rather than a home with human beings living and growing and interacting it could be a window display for an upscale retailer. Kimberly's gaze returned to Alicia. Through the film of tears she saw a soul desperately clinging to a moment. Alicia was unable to let go. Something powerful was pulling her in a direction that the others could not understand. There was an emptiness that longed to be filled, a sadness that lay beneath the surface for too long, and a spirit that had lost hope. For whatever reason, she and her father stirred emotions and desires and maybe even hope in someone. Kimberly spoke directly to Alicia, "One time I heard a symphony. It was different and beautiful. At times intense, then gentle. It was mysterious, yet common. The use of instruments went from melodic mixes to unexpected dissonant challenges. It was thrilling. I really liked it. Someone on the bus was playing it on an MP3 player with speakers. The bus was crowded and I couldn't get to them to ask what it was. For all I know it was their composition. They got off and I've never heard that music again or been able to find out what it was or who composed it. It left me with an empty feeling of loss and sadness. I may never hear that wonderful music again."

"You are that wonderful music," Alicia cried out.

"Now, Alicia," Shaun spoke up. "They have their own lives and want to get back on their way."

Alicia ignored her husband and spoke with Kimberly, "I'm not asking you to stay and give up your tour. All I ask is for some way for us to stay connected. I know it's a lot to ask to let strangers into your life."

"Maybe they can send us some postcards," Shaun said which resulted in an icy stare from his wife.

Indiana walked over to Alicia. He put his arm around Kimberly and said, "I don't know that we are ready for any new relationships, right now. We're still finding ourselves. In the long run it wouldn't be fair to you. Our single focus has to be on the tour. After that—who knows."

"Let's talk about the tour," Alicia said.

"There's not much to talk about," Indiana started. "The big truck is facing that way so we will start by going that way and then let the wind blow us to another destination."

"I want to help with the tour," Alicia stated emphatically.

"Alicia, stop," Shaun ordered.

"People on tour usually have a bus or RV—not a big truck."

"I like my truck," Indiana replied.

"But is it the best thing for Kimberly?" Alicia asked.

"She likes my truck."

Kimberly coughed.

"I want to make you an offer," Alicia began.

"What?" a surprised Shaun blurt out. "What offer?"

"We will buy an RV and rent it to you for one dollar a year."

"Ali . . ." Shaun stopped when he saw the look on his wife's face. She looked more alive than he had seen in years. Even in a blue bathrobe and fuzzy slippers she looked beautiful. There was an energy emanating from her that told him this was something she really wanted. He loved her and his heart melted. They had money and could afford it. Well, with the new contract and if they didn't take a vacation this year it could be done. He wondered if he could write it off as a business expense. Shaun looked at Indiana and said, "I'd take the deal before she sobers up."

"Listen, that's very generous, but we can't accept such an offer," Indiana stated.

It was Shaun's turn to get involved, "Indiana, we can afford it. It's not pity or charity. Think of us as patrons of the arts." He glanced at Kimberly, "Miss Kimberly is a talented musician who is sharing her music with people who will appreciate it. It will simply be a more enjoyable tour if you are comfortable."

"It's out of the question," Indiana insisted.

"When you offered to drive me to that meeting, yesterday, you didn't have an ulterior motive. You were simply in a position to help and you did. As a result, I got a fat contract worth a great deal. Now, we are in a position to help with the tour. It's that simple."

"It's not the same thing," Indiana protested.

"Sure it is." Shaun added with a smile, "Besides, after you backed into my car and half destroyed it—you owe me."

Light laughter filled the room.

Kimberly walked over to the window and looked out. She said to nobody in particular, "I like the blue whale." Indiana nodded in her direction to indicate that the subject was closed. The twelve-year-old then turned to face the three adults and said, "It is a bit cramped."

Alicia quickly stated, "An RV would give you more room, better sleeping quarters, a kitchen . . ."

"A shower," Shaun interjected, raising an eyebrow.

Alicia asked, "How do you practice in the cab of that truck?"

"We manage," Indiana answered. "Listen, I appreciate the offer. Under different circumstances we might accept it. But, we just don't need any entanglements or new responsibilities, at this time. Besides, what would I do with the big truck?"

"Leave it where it is or park it in my driveway," Shaun offered. "I'd buy an RV just for the pleasure of doing that."

"I'm sorry, no," Indiana said.

Shaun said softly to his wife, "Alicia, it's time to let go."

After a period of silence where only a drip in the sink could be heard, Alicia began, "Indiana, I've been a pain-in-the-ass during your entire visit. Forgive me for being overly-concerned and overly-zealous. I simply wasn't prepared to meet someone like Kimberly, or to hear your story, or to come face-to-face with my own inadequacies. We don't have any children and I guess I figuratively tried to steal yours. I wanted so much to hear how you are doing, to share the adventure, to keep hearing her music, and to help. It was wrong of me to step in where I really don't belong." She walked over and grasped Indiana's hand, then ended by saying, "The offer stands. I won't pressure you anymore. It would be wonderful if you accepted it, but I fully understand if you do not."

Alicia turned her attention to Kimberly, "You are a beautiful young lady with so much talent, and it has been an honor meeting and hearing you. It might sound odd but I will miss you after only knowing you for a single day."

"Nice act," Kimberly observed in a hushed voice.

"Did it work?" Alicia asked with a smile.

"Not sure."

CHAPTER 7

Once Kimberly was convinced, it was only a matter of finding the right land yacht. Therefore, four shoppers visited three RV dealers. At the third one they looked at an RV that was built on a Ford full-size van chassis. It had an extended wheelbase and dual wheels on the rear. Inside were accommodations for five people, if needed. There were two queen size beds—one in the rear of the vehicle and the other above the cab.

As had been the routine at the previous two dealerships, Shaun and Indiana waited outside as Kimberly and Alicia explored the vehicle.

"You realize that I am still not in favor of this," Indiana admitted.

"I know," was all Shaun replied.

"I don't even know what I'm going to do with the tractor and trailer." Indiana removed his hat and ran his hand through his hair, "It just doesn't make any sense."

"I have a solution for that." Shaun said, "Leave it in my driveway. I'd love to stir things up in our happy little development." After a pause he continued, "Seriously, we have a warehouse at my business where you can park the big truck."

"It's not that easy," Indiana protested, "You have to run the engine regularly to keep all of the parts lubricated. And it needs to be moved to keep the tires and brakes from deteriorating. Not to mention the drivetrain, transmission, and clutch." He shook his head, "You just can't leave it sitting."

"OK, here's what you do," Shaun advised, "Tell Alicia

you will only accept her proposal if she agrees to take care of the truck. That means running the engine and moving it around the parking lot on a regular basis. You set the schedule." Shaun couldn't help but smile thinking of Alicia's reaction.

"She doesn't know how to drive a truck."

"She can learn."

"She'll wreck it."

"No, she's a good driver," Shaun offered. "Besides, she'll probably get to like it. It'll get her out of the house. Maybe, she could start a whole new career."

Alicia and Kimberly exited the van RV. "It's perfect," Alicia said enthusiastically. "There are two beds, a kitchen, bathroom," she turned to look at Kimberly, "and shower, television, table and lots of storage space."

"Alicia, Indiana has a concern," Shaun stated.

"Oh, please don't say no, now. You already agreed."

"He's concerned about his truck," Shaun continued. "Someone has to start the engine and drive it around on a regular basis or else the whole thing will cease-up and become a massive paperweight."

"Well," Alicia answered, "you can do that."

"I'll be too busy with the new contract and existing projects."

"Well, I can't do it. I've never driven a truck."

"OK, that settles it," Indiana said as seriously as he could, "We continue the tour in the big truck."

"No!" Alicia protested, "I can learn to drive it."

"Are you sure?" asked Shaun.

"No, yes, I don't know, but I'll try."

Kimberly walked over to her father. She said in a low voice, "You and Mr. Harper have been conspiring."

"Is it obvious?"

"It always is."

"Right."

"What are we going to do?" Kimberly asked.

"What do you want to do?"

"It does have a shower. And, will be much more fuel efficient. It will be easier to park." Kimberly took her father's hand and led him into the RV. Together they explored the vehicle. As they did Kimberly said, "Don't be too rough on Mrs. Harper. There's something more going on than we realize."

Eventually, they sat at the table in the RV. Indiana looked at the comfortable surroundings and direct entry to the cab. He knew it would be a great deal more pleasant for Kimberly than being cooped up in the Kenworth. He also knew the RV was what she wanted.

"What do you think?" Kimberly asked. "Do you think you can handle a rig this big?"

Indiana laughed. The smile on Kim's face and her undaunted spirit always warmed his heart. It also saddened him as he wanted to give her everything he could, but there were limitations. Finally he expressed his concern, "It's beautiful and would make the tour far more comfortable. However, there are economic realities that we have to face. You know we make money doing short hauls when we stop in different cities. Without the Kenworth we won't have that income opportunity. The money we have from the sale of the house and our savings will only take us so far. A rough guess is that we could go eight to ten months. Then the tour ends."

"I see," Kimberly said considering the facts.

The double entente of her use of the word "see" struck Indiana. He might have financial limitations but her ability to see was also limited. Maybe in eight months without the short hauls they could cover more ground, see more sights, and improve the tour. If he sold his truck they could go another year. At that point the tour might end. However, if he had anything to do with it they would be the most jammed packed twenty months known to man or violinist.

"How about this," Kimberly offered, "we go six months. Pay the Harpers fifty cents." She smiled and shrugged, "Then we come back here and get big blue."

"How about, we go the limit. Take our chances. We put aside just enough to get back to big blue. When that time comes we face it. Until then, the tour continues."

"Are you sure?"

"Heck no. But, can we be sure of anything?"

The door opened and Alicia and Shaun entered. "See its lovely," Alicia commented.

"Very nice," Shaun added as he looked around.

Alicia spoke to Indiana, "We discussed the situation and I'm ready to become a truck driver."

"The question is; is my truck ready to be driven by you."

That afternoon, after unhooking the trailer, the driving lessons began in a quiet upscale neighborhood. Indiana showed Alicia how to start the engine explaining that with diesel you have to turn the key on and wait. Glow plugs heat the air in the engine which allows the fuel to ignite. When the "Wait to Start" light goes out it is time to start the engine. They got past that step quickly which was when everything fell apart. The art of double clutching is not that difficult, once mastered. Unfortunately, it is like learning to ride a bicycle. When fear is introduced into the equation nothing good happens. After an hour and not moving an inch they decided to take a break.

"That didn't go well," Alicia admitted.

"It didn't go at all is more accurate," Indiana added.

"I know to start in second gear because first is used for starting up a hill and when the tachometer passes two thousand RPMs it's time to shift to the next gear." Alicia said proudly.

"That's great," Indiana said, "Now all we have to do is get you to put it in gear."

"I'll show you how," Kimberly offered unexpectedly.

Before Shaun could protest, Indiana tossed the keys to Kimberly. After fifteen minutes the big blue truck drove off.

When Shaun saw them leave he asked, "Should they be doing that?"

"Absolutely not. A minor and an unlicensed commercial driver? Now, there's a combination. If your HOA people knew, the cops would be here in two minutes."

"What do we do?"

"Wait."

"Aren't you worried?"

"About my clutch—yes."

After a short period of time the two men, who sat in the living room small talking, heard the air horn on the truck. Two short blasts announced their arrival. The telephone rang. When Shaun answered the call he explained that the big truck would be leaving shortly. He added that they would pay for the bush on the corner that got inadvertently crushed. He ended the call by stating emphatically that they were mistaken. It couldn't have been Alicia driving the truck.

Alicia and Kimberly entered the house.

Kimberly tossed the keys to her father and said, "We have a plan."

CHAPTER 8

Kimberly outlined the plan that she and Alicia had developed in a short ten minute truck driving lesson. They would plot on a map ten destinations. Each week Indiana and Kimberly would arrive at a location in each destination in time to perform a Thursday evening concert. It might be at a school, church, mall, park, or other performance space. The concert would be for charity, therefore arranged through a charity, with the organization keeping two-thirds of the receipts. If the audiences were large enough the plan would help fund the tour.

"It's a nice idea, sweetie," Indiana explained, "but, it takes a lot of planning and organization to schedule and do a benefit."

"That's where Alicia comes in," Kimberly answered as she looked at her co-conspirator.

"I will do all of the arranging, coordinating, and detail work," Alicia chimed in. "It will take time and the first few concerts will be small. Although, I believe in time, as word gets out, that you will develop a following which in turn will generate larger and larger audiences."

"Whoa, this is starting to sound like a business—way too complicated," Indiana protested.

"The only thing you and Kimberly will have to do is be at an agreed upon place on Thursday nights," Alicia explained.

"Even that! Remember? No schedules, no destinations, that was the Spit In Eye Tour," Indiana retorted.

"About that, dad," Kimberly interjected.

"About what?"

"The name."

"What about the name?"

"We have to change it."

"Why?"

"Because, it's too negative."

Indiana stood up and left the room. Shaun, Alicia, and Kimberly remained in the living room. At first there was silence. Then Alicia said, "Maybe, I should go and talk with him."

"No," Kimberly said softly, "He's thinking. It is a lot to swallow all at once."

"I seem to have this innate ability to upset people," Alicia confessed.

"You can't blame him," Shaun concluded, "In two days we have interfered with everything, forced ourselves into their lives, and upset all their plans."

Alicia started to reply, but instead remained silent and looked down at her hands. Shaun was correct in his assessment of the situation. She wondered how wanting to do something good could turn out being so difficult and painful. Shaun stood and walked over to his wife. He patted her softly on the shoulder and left the room.

In the kitchen Shaun found Indiana looking out the window. He asked, "Have they started picketing the big truck yet?"

Indiana exhaled releasing a slight, almost imperceptible, laugh, "When I'm coming down a steep hill in the rain and traffic abruptly stops in front of me—I know what to do. If a brake hangs up—I know how to handle it. With Kimberly it's all new territory. I want to be fair. I want to be a good father. I want the best for her. I can't change the past or remove the struggle the lays ahead. What I can do is try to make the best decisions that I can that will benefit her, protect her, and bring her the most happiness. I just don't know if filling her head with fancy ideas is appropriate at this time. She's had enough disappointment."

"When you arrived at our house and Kimberly entered carrying her violin case I know you didn't see the shock in Alicia's eyes," Shaun said. "I did." Indiana turned to look at Shaun, who continued, "About five years ago Alicia had an automobile accident. Since then, she hasn't been the same." Shaun looked at the door that led to the living room as if making sure the ladies wouldn't overhear what he was going to say next. "She was driving down a side street downtown. A seven year old girl ran out from between two parked cars. Alicia had no time to stop. She barely was able to hit the brakes and turn the steering wheel. It wasn't enough. She hit and killed that little girl. Lying next to the child was a broken violin case and a shattered violin."

"My God," Indiana whispered.

"Alicia has never been the same. She was cleared of any fault in the accident, but that didn't help. Up until then we had discussed having children. Those talks stopped. Alicia was once filled with life and optimism. Not after that tragic day. She became introverted and nervous. In addition, she's become over protective of every child she sees. Somehow she's trying to keep any more terrible accidents from happening. In my opinion, Alicia was the other victim of that accident."

"The child was seven, you say?"

"Yes. She would be twelve-years-old today."

"The same as Kimberly."

"Whatever forces brought us together, Alicia believes it is her opportunity to make up for the harm that she did."

"Did she tell you that?"

"No. We never discuss the accident. That's my conclusion. Her enthusiasm is something that I haven't seen in five years. I believe she sees in Kimberly the music that she silenced so long ago. I don't think she will ever completely get over the guilt, but I know she can find value in her life once more."

From the living room they heard a violin. It played the hauntingly beautiful Sibelius *Concerto in D Minor*. The tones and notes seemed to reflect conflict that lived within the walls of this home. As the music reached out to each occupant they faced their own private thoughts and feelings. Note after note swirled around them. Emotions stirred. The power of music on the human psyche caused each listener to see things more clearly. So much had passed among them in two short days. Yet they each knew one undeniable truth. Whatever forces did bring them together also forged a bond that wouldn't be broken. The music increased in tempo and energy as if sleighing down a snow covered hill into an unknown future. They were committed and the music would guide them. Each individual involved might someday look back on the events of these two days and be amazed at what transpired. In one way or another they all had changed. The music stopped.

A harsh silence prevailed. It was almost painful in effect after the hypnotic spell of the violin.

"The Black Ice Tour," Indiana finally said.

"Excuse me?" Shaun replied.

"If you hadn't been so careless and nearly destroyed my truck after sliding on black ice that any driver who was paying attention would have seen we wouldn't have come to this point."

"So, I'm to blame."

"It looks that way to me."

"Black Ice Tour," Shaun said, "It does have a nice ring. Does that mean you are onboard with the plan?"

"If it is what Kimberly wants and Alicia can make it happen, I'm willing to try. If it also helps Alicia then it's the right thing to do. I don't know how I would deal with such an accident, myself. What a turn of events that our paths should cross." Indiana said.

"One thing," Shaun said, "we don't have to bring up the accident. I'm not even sure Alicia has made the connection and I don't want to open old wounds."

"From what you told me, I'm sure she has relived that accident and felt the pain once again. I won't say anything, but she knows why you came in here and what you have revealed to me."

When the two men returned to the living room they found Alicia and Kimberly looking at a map. Before Indiana could say a word, Shaun asked, "Planning the Black Ice Tour?"

"Black Ice Tour," Alicia said as if trying to picture it in her mind, "I like it." She looked at Kimberly and asked, "What do you think?"

"It's better than 'spit in eye' and is a little mysterious. I like it too. Good name, Mr. Harper."

Indiana punched Shaun on the arm.

CHAPTER 9

Events started happening quickly. They purchased and took delivery of the Ford RV, which Kimberly named Mozart. Alicia was given additional lessons and actually began to enjoy driving the blue Kenworth T700. More than once, she blew the distinctive air horn when in front of the home of a member of the Homeowners' Association. Then the telephone rang at the Harper residence. Shaun answered, listened, and then hung up.

"The hornets are really stirred up," he told Indiana who sat in the living room reviewing the RV owner's manual.

"She better be careful. She doesn't have a commercial license," Indiana warned.

"What do you bet she decides to get one?"

"Tell you what, I'll rent her the Kenworth for a dollar a year."

"I'm afraid she might take you up on it," Shaun replied with a smile.

"How do you feel about all of this?" Indiana asked Shaun unexpectedly.

Shaun thought for a moment. He then walked over to Indiana and sat opposite him. "At first, I was concerned with Alicia's meddling. Then I saw a change in her. It made me feel hopeful. It's hard to explain. When you see someone you love fold up and pull inside and become disconnected from the world it breaks your heart and tests your strength. We've been living in limbo. And, maybe we were drifting apart. You can't remain emotionally distant without it taking a toll."

"Then you slammed into my truck."

"And, Alicia met Kimberly."

"And, this crazy whirlwind of events took place."

"It's almost out-of-control."

"Almost?"

"OK, you and I have no control. But, those two ladies are planning, conspiring, and making things happen."

"Maybe, they are good for each other."

"They are," Shaun stated, then added, "I know Kimberly has already had an effect on Alicia. She is energized, involved, and . . . happy. What about Kimberly?"

"There are times that I'm not sure what she is thinking or feeling. This is not one of those times. Kimberly likes Alicia. That is obvious. However, there is also a deeper connection between them that neither you nor I see."

"It makes you wonder about this kismet thing."

"Destiny, predestination, kismet, whatever you call it, there was a reason for them to come together."

"Black Ice," Shaun said in a thoughtful manner. "Was that the divine method that caused us to meet?"

"Or, your lousy driving," Indiana offered.

"No, can't be that." Shaun stood and walked over to the mantel and picked up a hockey trophy and examined it. "I used to be good on ice."

"Scotch is good on ice."

Shaun smiled but then got a pensive look as he handled the trophy, "Sometimes I feel guilty."

Indiana didn't reply.

"Things have come easy for me. I haven't faced the same trials and tribulations as Alicia or Kimberly or you. My life has been one success after another. There haven't been setbacks or pain. It makes me wonder how I would handle adversity. Much like someone who has never been in a fight, they don't know if they can take a punch. I have a big house, enough money, a beautiful wife, my health, a successful business, good looks . . ."

Indiana coughed.

"I'm not ugly."

"I picked you up, if you recall."

Shaun smiled then continued, "Somehow, I feel like I haven't paid my dues. Why should I have everything fall into my lap and then a talented child, like Kimberly, have so many terrible things happen at such a young age?"

"I've asked myself the same question," Indiana admitted. "The only thing I can come up with is that it basically is chance. On a scale of good and bad things most people fall close to the middle while there are always those at the extremes. It's luck—good and bad."

They heard the truck pull up in front of the house. The air horn announced its arrival. When the front door of the house opened Shaun and Indiana heard laughter. Alicia and Kimberly entered the living room. Kimberly walked over to her father and said, "We have our first destination."

"Oh, where are we headed?" Indiana asked.

"It's a surprise."

"How are we going to get there if I don't know where to go?"

"I'm going to be the navigator."

"We think it is the perfect start to the Black Ice tour," chimed in Alicia.

Indiana punched Shaun on the arm.

While rubbing his arm Shaun asked, "Shouldn't we get things prepared? We need to park the truck at the warehouse, purchase supplies for Mozart, and get them on the road."

"Before that, Kimberly and I have to go shopping," Alicia stated.

"What now?" asked Shaun.

"She needs some dresses and shoes and I want to get her hair done."

"Of course."

Indiana wanted to protest and say that they had done enough. The excited look on Kimberly's face kept him silent. He noted a definite change in his daughter which gave him hope. As a father he could protect her, feed her, and advise her. What he couldn't do was give her the kind of support and guidance that a woman could provide. While his pride was bruised he welcomed the opportunity for Kimberly to have a "female" influence.

"Don't take too long," Shaun warned, "they have to get on the road."

"There's plenty of time. The first performance isn't that far away," Alicia offered. "Besides, I need at least one more driving lesson."

"Just stop tweaking the noses of the Homeowner's Association members."

The doorbell rang. When Shaun opened the door he found himself face to face with two police officers.

CHAPTER 10

"Mr. Harper?" the taller police officer asked.

"Yes, how can I help you?" Shaun replied knowing darn well why they were there.

"We've had complaints of a blue truck riding around the neighborhood disturbing the peace, damaging property, and supposedly being driven by an unlicensed driver," the police officer stated, then asked, "Would you know anything about that?"

Shaun knew better than to lie. It would only make things worse and could lead to additional charges. He also knew the complaints weren't that severe and the whole thing could be easily resolved. He replied, "I do. If you would join me in the kitchen I will be happy to explain everything." The two police officers followed Shaun.

When the three men entered the kitchen the taller officer stated firmly, "This may not sound like much but it is a very serious matter. If someone had been injured the consequences would be far-reaching and severe. It could be assault with a deadly weapon, reckless endangerment, and if a victim died—manslaughter."

At first Shaun was caught off guard by the officer's attitude.

Officer Austin continued, "In addition, the perpetrator could have their driver's license suspended, be charged with driving without a license," he added as an aside, "commercial license, endangering a child, willful destruction of property, harassment, terrorism . . ."

"Terrorism?"

"Yes, terrorism. Driving around in a huge vehicle and

threatening neighbors fits the definition."

"Well, I wouldn't go that far," Shaun started.

"Mr. Harper," Officer Austin took his handcuffs out of his pocket and held them out for effect, "I can place the perpetrator under arrest—right now."

"The perpetrator is my wife. And, if you give me a few moments, I will explain everything."

"Maybe, we should be having this conversation with your wife."

"I'd prefer to discuss it with you first, if you don't mind."

"Mr. Harper, where is your wife?"

Shaun hesitated as he tried to formulate a strategy to allow him to explain the situation before bringing Alicia into it. He was trying to protect her. There had been such a wonderful change in Alicia that he didn't want to destroy it.

From the den violin music drifted into the kitchen. Kimberly played Samuel Barber's *Adagio for Strings, op. 11.* It's slow and tender emotional tones entered softly bringing silence to the room. The two police officers looked at each other, then toward Shaun. Nothing was said as they listened to a young girl's musical message. The melodic grip held firm. Each man found his thoughts wandering to distant recesses of their mind to relive moments from their past. Time ceased. More than musical notes reached out to them. The essence of human emotion engulfed each soul.

Finally, the shorter, more rotund, and older officer said almost in a whisper, "I know that music. Four days after 9/11 the BBC Orchestra played it in honor of those who lost their lives."

When the playing ended, the taller officer said in a more friendly tone to Shaun, "Tell us about what happened."

As Shaun gave a dissertation on the events of the past few days Vaughan Williams, *Fantasia on a Theme* filled the air. The mood in the kitchen became more upbeat. Both police officers nodded as they listened and even laughed when Shaun told how they forced Alicia to agree to learn to drive the "big truck."

When Shaun finished, the shorter office, named Ignatius Teal, said, "I think we have all we need. Without seeing your wife behind the wheel we really don't have any case." He looked in the direction of the den and added, "I'd like to meet your wife and this young lady."

The three men entered the den quietly as Kimberly continued to play. Her eyes were closed so she didn't know that they had entered the room. Lost in her world she continued her journey with unexplainable ease. Officer Teal nonchalantly wiped a tear from his eye hoping his partner wouldn't notice.

When Kimberly finished, she opened her eyes and became aware of the new arrivals. "Hello," she immediately said adding, "are you going to arrest us?"

Officer Teal shook his head unable to speak for a moment. Quickly, he regained his composure and replied, "No. We see no reason for any legal action." He turned toward Alicia and said, "However, we don't want any more complaints about you, or some other unknown woman, driving a commercial vehicle on city streets without a proper license."

Alicia nodded.

"But there's a bush out there that . . .," Everyone turned toward Kimberly who stated, "Never mind."

Officer Teal asked Kimberly, "That first piece that you played."

"Adagio"

"Yes, why did you play that piece?"

"I don't know. It just came to me."

"You did a wonderful job."

"Thank you."

Officer Teal turned his attention to the room in general and said, "So, tell me about this tour."

"Black Ice Tour," Kimberly added.

"Yes, the Black Ice Tour. When does it start and where are you going?"

"Actually," Alicia answered, "the first concert is going to be right here in our neighborhood community center on Thursday evening."

"Surprise," Kimberly said to her father.

"Have arrangements already been made?" Indiana asked.

"I spoke to Hannah McBride who is in charge and the venue is available," Alicia answered.

"How available?" Shaun asked.

"Completely available."

"How available?" he repeated.

"We have the community house from five to ten."

"How available?"

"We only have to make sure to clean up afterwards."

"How much?" Shaun changed the question.

"Five Hundred Dollars."

Shaun looked at Officer Austin, the taller policeman, and asked, "Can I borrow your gun?"

Officer Austin didn't answer, but Officer Teal did with a smile, "You can't shoot her."

"It's for me," Shaun stated.

"Listen, it's for charity," Alicia explained as she stood and walked over to stand beside Kimberly. "We ask for donations and should more than cover the cost."

"How do we know that anybody will attend?" Indiana asked.

"That's where the charity comes in. They have two days

to invite everyone on their email list to a free concert."

"Which charity is doing this?" Shaun asked.

"Well . . ." Alicia didn't have an answer.

"You don't have one, do you?"

"Officer," Kimberly said to Officer Teal, "Do the police have a charity?"

"We have a number of charities," he responded, "Patrolman's Benevolent Association, Police Athletic League, DARE, Fallen Officer's Foundation."

"Why don't we do the concert to support those organizations?" Kimberly suggested.

"Well, I don't know," Officer Teal replied. "I don't even know who would make such a decision. It doesn't seem like something that is possible in such a short period of time. I'm at a loss"

"Welcome to the club," Shaun stated flatly.

Officer Teal looked at Shaun, then Alicia, then Indiana, and finally Kimberly. Kimberly did a quick rendition of the theme from *Rocky* on her violin, shrugged, and smiled. A reciprocal smile spread across his face and he said, "OK, I'll see what I can do."

"The charity gets two thirds of the profit," Alicia explained.

The two police officers told Kimberly that they enjoyed her playing and agreed to pursue the charities. Once Shaun, Alicia, Kimberly, and Indiana were alone they began to plan the upcoming concert. What they didn't know was what was going to happen on Thursday night.

CHAPTER 11

Thursday night came very quickly. Too quickly to suit Shaun who felt there wasn't ample time for people to become aware of the concert or to make plans. Outside the community house a light snow fell, further dampening his hopes. Shaun, Alicia, and Indiana had made sure all chairs were set up, refreshments for the intermission ready, and the all-important donation jar was strategically placed near the door. There was nothing left to do but wait.

Information pertaining to the concert had been sent to specified contacts at different police oriented charities, the media, and the Harper's neighbors. It stated that the free concert would run from 7:00 p.m. to 9:00 p.m. This would allow them an hour to clean up afterwards. At 6:30 p.m. no one had arrived. At that time there was no reason for concern as very few people ever arrive a half hour early.

"This snow isn't going to help," Shaun concluded.

"At least it's not ice," Indiana answered.

"It could be black ice," Shaun countered.

"This is Black Ice," Indiana waved his arm to encompass the room. "That is a dusting of snow."

They heard music from a back room where Kimberly was warming up. In silence, Alicia stood by a window looking out. She so wanted the room to be filled with people who would enjoy the music as much as she had. Yet, she knew this was a test. If they didn't make it work, would that mean the whole Black Ice Tour was a mistake? If no one showed up, how would Kimberly feel? The click of a front door being opened jarred Alicia from her thoughts. She turned and saw a woman and a seven-year-old girl enter the community house. The young girl carried a violin case. Alicia gasped in surprise. This couldn't be happening. Was she being haunted, or punished, or was she lost in a bad dream? The mother and daughter walked up the aisle and sat in the front row. Alicia looked at her watch. It was 6:50 p.m. She decided that she had to tell Kimberly about the disappointing turnout, or more accurately non-turnout.

Alicia entered the small room where Kimberly was putting rosin on her bow. The soloist wore a deep-blue silk jersey dress with long sleeves. It had a layered hemline just below the knee. She wore round toe black pumps with two-inch heels and had her hair pulled back into a ponytail. Alicia looked at the twelve-year-old girl who looked remarkably grown up. They had gone shopping the day before and Alicia had told Kimberly not to mention to Shaun how much the dress and shoes had cost. When Kimberly saw Alicia she asked, "Is it time?"

Alicia hesitated and then said sadly, "I'm afraid we don't have an audience."

"No one came?" Kimberly asked not showing any emotion.

"There's a mother and daughter. That's all."

"Then we have an audience," Kimberly stood and picked up her violin.

"You can't play for just two people," Alicia said wanting to save Kimberly from the embarrassment.

"I played for you and Mister Harper."

"But, that was in a home not a performance space."

"Music doesn't require a certain number of listeners to have value. If I play alone the notes still exist in all their beauty and meaning and emotion. My love of the sounds, harmonics, cadence, intonation, and composition doesn't depend on who else is listening. If I play for one or one million it is the music that draws me in and speaks in languages that only it and I understand."

At that moment, Alicia realized that Kimberly approached the tour and performance from a completely different perspective. She played for the love of playing. She experienced the music more than she required an audience's approval. If there ever was someone who was a pure musician she was in the room with her. Finally, she said, "Then let the tour, no matter how humble, begin."

When Kimberly walked onto the stage she saw the mother and daughter sitting in the front row. She also saw the violin case. Without stopping she walked down the stage stairs and over to the two audience members. "Do you play violin?" she asked the young girl.

The seven-year-old's face lit up and she said, "Yes, but I'm not very good."

"Do you like playing?"

"Oh, yes."

"Then would you play for me?"

The girl looked at her mother who smiled and nodded. Kimberly then took the girl's hand and led her onto the stage. Indiana brought out an extra chair. When they were seated Kimberly said, "My name is Kimberly. What's yours?"

"Andrea."

"Well, Andrea, what song can you play?"

"We only learned how to plink."

Kimberly took Andrea's violin and quickly tuned it. As she handed it back to the child she asked, "Why don't you show me what you play?"

Andrea started plucking the strings and the tune *Twinkle Twinkle Little Star* could be recognized. When she finished, Kimberly said, "Very good. Now do it again and I'll play with you." When Andrea started plucking the strings

Kimberly played a soft melody in the background. The combination was surprisingly interesting and moving. When they finished the little girl's mouth was wide open and she turned toward her mother and yelled, "Mommie, did you see? I want to play like her someday."

"Now, do you want to try something harder?" Kimberly asked.

Andrea nodded and Kimberly showed her a number of notes to pluck. It took a few tries before the seven-year-old violinist got the notes right. When Kimberly was satisfied she told Andrea to stand and face the audience and play. The child plucked the notes and Kimberly accompanied her. Together they played Robert Schumann's *The Merry Peasant*. When they finished Kimberly looked up and saw four more people had joined the audience.

"I wish I could play with that," Andrea pointed at Kimberly's bow.

"Well, let's see what we can do." Kimberly removed her spare bow from her case and handed it to Andrea. It took a while and some work to get Andrea to hold the bow correctly. With encouragement and guidance Kimberly was able to teach the younger violinist how to move the bow across the strings to generate a clear note. She then taught Andrea how to go from one string to another. The lesson ended with the two playing a simple tune that didn't require pressing strings on frets. Andrea's mother was astonished seeing her daughter play the violin as she did. Kimberly thanked Andrea and led her back to her seat.

Without introduction or saying a word Kimberly stood on the stage and began the evening with *La Capricieuse Op.17* by Edward Elgar. It brought a light and airy tone to the evening. She then introduced energy with Vivaldi's *Four Seasons Winter*. A variety of Johann Sebastian Bach Violin

Concertos were next. Finally, Kimberly ended the first hour with the Mendelssohn *Violin Concerto in E minor, Op. 64.* When she finished and looked up to her surprise there were over a hundred persons in the audience. She smiled as she felt the warmth of their applause.

During the intermission Kimberly spoke with numerous audience members. The snow had caused many to be late, while changing police shifts accounted for others' tardiness. She heard again and again how amazed they were that she didn't use music when she played. As it turned out the evening was a total success. More and more latecomers arrived and enjoyed an outstanding performance. At 9:00 p.m. when the concert was to end the audience kept asking for more. At 9:30 p.m. Alicia announced that they had to stop because they only had the venue until ten and had to clean up. A woman in the audience stood and offered, "We'll help clean up, if Kimberly would play while we do."

In the end they raised over three thousand dollars with two thousand going to the police oriented charities. Alicia and Kimberly were delighted with the outcome.

Indiana stood on the sidelines wondering where all of this was going to lead. He knew they were about to embark on a great adventure. He also knew they were racing time.

Shaun found a note in the donation jar that read: I'm beginning to like the big truck.

CHAPTER 12

Over the next few months the Black Ice tour continued. Father and daughter traveled south chasing the warm sun. Kimberly played her violin in churches, community houses, libraries, college auditoriums, restaurants, hospitals, and more. Audience size varied and was completely unpredictable. However, the music and its creator were always well-received. Most importantly, different charities were beneficiaries and the tour remained solvent.

While driving from one venue to another Indiana and Kimberly were able to make side trips to see the sights and meet people. The tour was filling her head with a plethora of pictures and her heart with joy. Mozart, the Ford RV, proved to be far more comfortable and convenient than the big truck. Generally, they spoke with Shaun and Alicia at the beginning of each week to finalize plans for the Thursday night performance.

At one performance destination there were numerous horse farms with long white wooden fences, barns, and large expensive homes. Thoroughbreds of every size and color dotted pastures, were being led by grooms, or ridden on trails. Green lush countryside added to the beauty.

That evening Kimberly played in a barn. It was an elegant barn built, not for horses, but for horse people. The inside was a huge meeting space with hardwood floors, a stage, complete commercial kitchen, and private meeting rooms upstairs. The acoustics were exceptional. Indiana and Kimberly found that there was something warm and friendly about the atmosphere of the barn. People were welcoming and polite. Laughter filled the air as they prepared for the performance. The charity being helped, not surprisingly, was to support a wild horse sanctuary.

Kimberly walked onto the stage at eight o'clock. The room was filled to capacity. A din of conversation ceased when she appeared. Here and there she heard a cough. Then a quiet wave of anticipation flowed across the room. Suddenly, in the silence Kimberly heard her mother's voice. The words were not clear, but it was her mother and long buried emotions came to the surface. Kimberly closed her eyes and began to play. It was not the music she had planned. It was not a piece anyone had composed. Immediately, Indiana knew that his daughter was lost in her world of thoughts. He didn't know that mother and daughter were reaching out to each other. Slow and haunting tones filled the barn touching many in the audience. High notes gave the impression of a wailing child lost and afraid. A few had tears well up in their eyes. In the end, when Kimberly finished there was an extended moment of silence followed by overwhelming applause.

To change the mood Kimberly played the first two movements of *Masquerade* by Aram Khachaturian. It was written in 1941 for a production of a play with the same name by Russian poet and playwright Mikhail Lermontov. The first movement is a lively waltz giving the impression of a party or ball. This was followed by a softer more pensive solo giving the impression of someone longing for love. Through her violin Kimberly Jones reached every member of the audience that night. A simple and sweet rendition of Frederic Chopin's *Nocturne Op.9 No.2* was next. She finished the first half of the concert with the complex and lively *Fantasy* by Stepan Grytsay.

During the intermission Kimberly and Indiana mingled with the audience. It had become their habit. People wanted to meet the musician and often had questions. Of course, her story preceded her when Alicia made arrangements. On this occasion a middle-aged woman with long blond hair, a fashionable red dress, expensive jewelry, and cowboy boots stopped Indiana and Kimberly. She smiled broadly, took Kimberly's hand, and stated emphatically, "I am going to make a ten thousand dollar donation, on one condition."

"That's very generous," Indiana said.

"What's the condition?" Kimberly asked.

"That you agree to have lunch at our farm tomorrow."

"Is your cooking that bad?" asked Kimberly.

The woman was caught off guard and at first didn't know how to take the remark. Then she laughed and said, "Honey, there's more to you than music, I see." She handed Kimberly a card. "My name is Constance Whitmore. People call me Connie. I do hope you accept my invitation." She smiled and added, "I don't do the cooking so you ought not worry."

The rest of the concert went on without a hitch. A large amount of money was raised for the designated charity, as well as the tour. Numerous members of the audience thanked Kimberly and invited her to return for another concert.

The next day Indiana found the farm where they were to have lunch. It was a sprawling estate with white fences, large pastures, a paddock, and track. They stopped at the entrance where there was a metal horse statue. Kimberly was fascinated with the statue. When viewed from one angle it looked like a white horse. From another angle the horse appeared to be black. A long dirt road led to a distant house. Below the horse statue was a metal sign with the name "Burning Oak Farm" engraved in it.

"These are sights I want to capture," Kimberly said.

"It is a beautiful area," Indiana agreed.

"I never knew that there were places like this."

They were greeted at the door by a butler who led them into a wood paneled parlor. Constance Whitmore entered through another door. She was casually dressed in a brocaded blouse and denim skirt. She took both of Kimberly's hands and said, "Welcome to Burning Oak."

"Where's the pool?" Kimberly asked.

Again, Constance was surprised by an unexpected question but regained her composure and answered, "Out back. I'll show you later."

Over lunch, which consisted of roasted pepper tomato soup and a choice of grilled steak with watercress sandwiches or roasted asparagus and fresh herb grilled cheese, they talked about music, horses, and other things.

"I can't tell you how much I enjoyed your playing, last night."

"Thank you."

"That first piece, what was it?"

Kimberly paused, then explained, "It was actually something that I made up at the moment."

"That was your composition? You are a composer?"

"Not really. Sometimes I feel music and just play what is in my head."

"It was very sad and moving. I must admit that I cried. It took me back to a time when my late husband and I were together. I heard his voice in your music. Does that seem strange?"

In almost a whisper Kimberly replied, "Not at all."

"I would love to have a recording of that music but from what you tell me one doesn't exist."

"No, I don't record my music."

"You should. For such music to just flow from your

mind is such a wonderful gift. It should be shared."

"It's personal," Kimberly stated.

"I understand. It was presumptuous of me to want to possess something as exquisite and meaningful as that. I feel honored to have heard it. Somehow, it's sad that others will not have the opportunity."

The subject became horses. Kimberly expressed how beautiful the horse farms were and how happy she was to have seen them. Constance was aware of Kimberly's fate and as a result had a renewed appreciation of all that surrounded her. "Do you ride?" she asked.

"No. I never have," Kimberly answered.

"Well, it's time that you do. What size shoe do you wear?"

"Uh, seven."

"I have a pair of boots that will fit you. They are handmade custom leather boots that turned out to be too big for me."

"So, I have big feet?"

"Why, of course, hasn't anyone told you?" Constance wasn't going to be caught off-guard again. The two laughed and Constance said to Indiana, "You will join us, Mr. Jones."

The boots were black with abstract red roses inlaid and stitched on the shaft. They looked brand new and expensive. Constance had a groom saddle and bring out three horses. Because Indiana had told her that he had ridden before she wasn't concerned with selection of a mount for him. With Kimberly she was far more discerning. After talking with the groom they decided that a black mare named Cleopatra was the best choice. She was gentle and obedient to the reins. An afternoon of riding easy tree-lined trails was a welcome change from riding the roads of America. Indiana and Connie got to know each other better and found that they had a lot in common. She was impressed with his horsemanship and he with her strength and confidence. Burning Oak was a large farm with many employees. Constance Whitmore made it work. By the end of the afternoon they were pleasantly fatigued. Kimberly's rear end was sore as she never mastered posting.

Back at the barn they dismounted and Constance asked Kimberly, "How did you like Cleopatra?"

"She was wonderful. A perfect choice. She is a beautiful horse."

"She's yours," Constance said.

Kimberly was caught off guard and sputtered, "Uh. . . what?"

"Lost for words, dear? She is a beautiful horse and a thoroughbred. You are an accomplished musician with talents even you don't realize. You belong together."

"We can't take a horse," Indiana said.

"Oh, she can live here as long as you wish. You can visit her and ride her whenever it suits you. She will be a welcome permanent guest."

Indiana looked over at Kimberly who was stroking Cleopatra and whispering to her. He knew the decision had been made. Like so many decisions lately he always found himself caught up in the flow not able to make a difference. Yet, Kimberly and Cleopatra made him smile.

"You're too generous," he told Constance.

She answered in a low voice, "Nonsense, that child deserves as much happiness as can be bestowed upon her."

Kimberly went past them which caused Indiana to ask, "Where are you going?"

"I want to see if Cleopatra likes music." She stopped and said to Constance, "You can tape it if you wish."

For half an hour Kimberly played and Cleopatra listened. She seemed fascinated with her new friend and whinnied a few times. A number of times it fit the music quite well.

Back inside the house Kimberly thanked Constance for being so kind and generous. She began to take off the cowboy boots but Constance said, "You keep them. They don't fit me."

"You've been far too generous," Indiana stated.

"I think I came out ahead on the deal," Constance held up the recorder that held one-of-a-kind violin music. "You can buy things, but a rare gift from the heart is priceless. I'm a good business woman but I know that fact all too well. You come back and see us anytime."

As they drove away, leaving Burning Oak, they were unprepared for what their next stop would bring.

CHAPTER 13

The Black Ice Tour took Indiana and Kimberly to a large city. A high school auditorium was the performance space. The charity that was the sponsor was the Inner City Reclamation Foundation. When they arrived for the Thursday night performance they were met by a nice, slightly overweight, middle-aged, black woman who introduced herself as Tiffany Dillmon. She was the executive director of the foundation and was beaming with excitement.

"How nice it is to have you perform for us this evening," Ms. Dillmon exclaimed.

"Thank you for giving me the opportunity," Kimberly replied.

"Our foundation raises money to improve the buildings in the inner city in order to attract businesses and create jobs. The funds you help us raise tonight will touch many lives." She led them to a classroom and said, "You can use this room to prepare. We have student volunteers helping us out this evening. If you need anything just ask any student with a yellow I.D. tag and they will help you."

The classroom brought back memories to Kimberly of not-so-pleasant days she spent in school. At the time, she didn't know why she was an outcast. To a young child being ridiculed and rejected hurt. She didn't understand that her outperforming older students and having a desire to learn made her a misfit. Now, with all that had transpired in her life she could understand on an intellectual level the dynamics of what happened. Yet, from an emotional perspective scars remained. Kimberly picked up her violin and played an introspective composition to clear her mind. In this case the music was desultory in nature going from powerful and dramatic to soft and pleading. Discordant notes sprang forth driven by anger, yet tempered by softer tones. Tempo changed unexpectedly. Strings strained to provide sounds demanded of them. Demons danced and angels sang in a conflict that would not be decided but would remain within a young girl who at times felt shredded by the turmoil. A tear escaped followed by others and the music cried along with her.

In the hallway Indiana heard Kimberly "thinking" and became alarmed. The intensity of the music was uncharacteristic of her. His first impulse was to go to his daughter to see what was wrong. However, something held him back. A father's inadequacy, painful and upsetting, sometimes leads to inaction. The desire to fix whatever is wrong is strong. Yet, in those instances where no solution is evident a desperate mental search ensues followed by hesitation. If Kimberly faced a physical threat Indiana would spring into action without delay. If someone was causing her distress he would handle it. A young girl's emotional struggles are a completely different story so foreign that they induce an overwhelming kind of fear. The wrong move and a delicate balance could be disrupted forever. He made a fist, angry at himself for not knowing what to do. His cheeks became moist and he turned toward the wall.

The music stopped.

When Indiana entered the classroom he found Kimberly placing her violin into its case. They made eye-contact. Kim seemed normal and composed. As she pressed a button on a recorder she said, "I don't think I'll send that one to Cleopatra."

"It might confuse her."

"This place. I'd forgotten," Kimberly ran her hand

across one of the student desks.

"Sometimes it's better to forget."

The concert that night went flawlessly. In attendance were the mayor and numerous other politicians and city officials. In their world it was necessary to be seen supporting the correct causes. Business people came with their spouses and those interested in the arts also attended. In addition, students from the school system were given free tickets.

Kimberly began with a tango, *La Cumparsita* for solo violin by G.M.Rodriges. Mozart's *Eine Kleine Nachtmusik* 3rd & 4th Movements followed. She then performed andante dolce of the solo violin *Sonata op.115* by Serguei Prokofiev. And, anyone who had attended a wedding was familiar with the next piece, Pachelbel's *Canon in D Major.* She finished the first half of the concert with a medley of Celtic folk music which left the audience energized.

The mayor approached Kimberly during the intermission and was careful to place himself in the best light for photographs by the media. While holding her hand he issued a statement, "This young lady is an inspiration for all of us to use our God-given talent to pursue our dreams. My dream for our city is to provide an educational system that brings out the best in all of our children whether it is in science or the arts or public service." He raised his arms bringing Kimberly's arm upward and striking a pose for the cameras as he proclaimed, "This is the launch of a reclaimed inner-city and renewal of our efforts to create a prosperous future for all of us!" Kimberly didn't know what to make of this blusterous, self-indulgent, media hog. She smiled and waited for her chance to break from the circus.

The second half of the program was a mix of soft tender melodies and intense dramatic pieces. She ended with *Flight of the Bumblebee* by Nikolai Rimsky-Korsakov which is a guaranteed crowd pleaser.   After the concert Kimberly returned to the classroom and placed her violin in its case. Some of the anxiety of being in a classroom had passed. The audience had been large and enthusiastic. Indeed, she had enjoyed playing on this evening.

Kimberly opened the door of the classroom and asked the student with a yellow I.D. that was watching the door where she could find the ladies room. It was down the hall on the left. As she walked down the hall she had the feeling once more of being a young child in a foreboding place. This was her graveyard in the middle of the night. Even though there were no ghosts lurking behind gravestones, there were ghosts in her mind. She knew she was letting her emotions get the best of her and that she had to regain control. The ladies room door was on her left and she paused to listen to hear if anyone else was in there. Silence. After a longer than usual pause she entered. The bathroom was empty.

As she was washing her hands two girls about her age entered the bathroom. They were joking and laughing. When they saw Kimberly they stopped.

The taller girl with long hair smiled and said, "You were awesome."

"Thank you."

"How did you ever learn to play that way?"

"Lots of practice."

"I knew that's what you'd say. That's what my mother always tells me."

"She's right." Kimberly felt uncomfortable in the small room with the two new arrivals.

"She's always right. That's what pisses me off."

Kimberly smiled.

The other girl who was heavier and wearing a sweatshirt with the school's mascot, a bulldog, on it said, "I tried learning piano but the practice was . . ." she made quotation marks in the air with her hands, "boring."

The taller girl asked, "Does your mother make you practice?"

"No."

"You got a boyfriend?"

"No."

"See, it's all that practice."

"I guess."

"I liked that song you did in the beginning—the tango."

"*La Cumparsita.*"

"I could see me and my boyfriend doing the tango. I'd wrap my legs around him."

"Yeah, and then you'd do that bumble bee thing," her friend remarked after which they both laughed.

Kimberly smiled and went to leave.

"Hey," the taller girl yelled, "you were awesome."

Awesome or awkward, Kimberly thought as she walked back up the hallway. She arrived at the classroom but the student who was standing at the door was no longer there. Quickly she entered the room and found it empty. Her jacket, purse, and violin were gone. Panic caused her to freeze. She looked around the room hoping to see her lost violin located elsewhere, but only empty desks remained.

She jumped when a hand touched her shoulder and Indiana asked, "Are you ready to go?"

"My violin," she turned to face her father, "it's gone!"

"Where was it? How did that happen?" he asked with a slight edge to his voice.

"I went to the ladies room."

"You left it here."

"There was a student watching the room."

"What did they say?"

"He wasn't here when I came back."

Kimberly fell into her father's arms and started to cry. Indiana stood comforting his daughter while his mind raced about what they needed to do next. Once more a father's inability to instantly fix what was wrong gnawed at him.

CHAPTER 14

After filling out police reports and answering numerous questions, Indiana and Kimberly were left sitting in an interview room in the local police station. It was then that Indiana called Shaun and Alicia. He told them what had occurred. They were both horrified and appropriately sympathetic. Alicia was the one who inquired how Kimberly was handling not having her violin "to think."

Kimberly, who was sitting next to her father, took the telephone and answered in a soft tone, "I guess I have to take off the training wheels sometime."

"We'll get you another violin," Alicia promised.

"You know, I really don't like schools," Kimberly responded. "Don't schedule any more schools."

"I won't."

"I hate schools," Kimberly said in a tone of voice that was harsh. "I hate this city. We should never have come here. It's ugly and depressing. I hate the stupid kid who stole my violin. I hate you for sending us here. I hate those girls in the bathroom. I hate this disease. I hate my mother for leaving me. And, I hate myself!"

Indiana sat in stunned silence. He'd never seen such an outburst from Kimberly. It concerned him and broke his heart. She was obviously in a great deal of pain—pain that had been building up for a long time hidden by notes and tones. A child's anger funneled into music was now forced to be expressed another way.

"Kimberly, you have a right to be angry and to hate all of those things, including me," Alicia said. "But, please, don't hate yourself because you are the only one who is innocent and pure and so truly wonderful."

"I'm a freak."

"You're a rare and remarkable human being—not a freak," Alicia stated in a soothing voice.

"I just don't fit in. Never have."

"You were given a gift of incredible talent."

"A gift that has a huge price tag."

"Yes, no one will deny that you have faced more than anyone your age should have to face. And, it's not fair. But, you've been trying to handle it all alone and, sweetheart, you are not alone. Your dad is there for you and he's smarter than you think." Kimberly reacted with a slight chuckle. Alicia continued, "Shaun and I are here and will do anything to help you. You know that. We are all on this adventure together. And in adventures good and bad things happen. You will smile again. And, you will swim among the musical notes again. And, people will experience music in ways they never expected again. The music hasn't stopped. We are simply turning the page." After a brief pause, Alicia said, "You may not know it but you've just stepped from childhood to adolescence and it will be a rocky road. Just ask my parents how many times I told them that I hate them."

"I'm sorry I said that," a calmer Kimberly replied.

"Don't be sorry. You had feelings that had to come out. There will be other feelings that you will have that you won't understand, but don't be afraid they are natural and in the end you will emerge as a beautiful, talented, exceptional woman."

Indiana sat in silence looking at his little girl. She wasn't so little, anymore. He thanked God for Alicia. She knew what to say and how to handle the situation. His mind drifted back to their first encounter in the Harper's kitchen. He wanted nothing more than to escape from Alicia. She forced herself into their lives. Overnight, all of their plans changed. He lost control and made fewer decisions. However, the tour turned out better than he could ever have imagined. And now, with this crisis, she was an anchor and surrogate mother that Kimberly needed.

A police detective entered the room so the telephone conversation ended. He told Indiana and Kimberly that it would take a few days for them to interview the student volunteers and others who had access to the classroom. Indiana agreed to remain in the area.

On the second day the police still didn't have any concrete leads to follow. The student that was at the classroom door was evasive but didn't admit to stealing the violin. An alert was issued to all pawn shops, music shops, and consignment stores. The detectives had to admit that in cases such as this there was quite often no positive outcome.

Indiana and Kimberly had visited a number of music stores in the area but none offered the level of quality instrument that they were looking for. Alicia was also on the hunt. She contacted orchestras, colleges with music programs, and well-known luthiers. In the end replacement of Kimberly's violin was going to be a difficult and expensive task.

Kimberly sat at the small table in their Ford RV. She was having trouble not being able to play her violin. A major part of her life was missing. She couldn't sleep, or eat, and found herself feeling lost and depressed.

A light tapping was heard on the RV. Indiana opened the door. An old man stood before him. He was short and slightly hunched over. Long grey hair hung down to his shoulders. Lines and creases on his face bespoke his advanced years. Dark brown eyes were slightly squinted as they looked directly at Indiana. His overcoat was clearly from a better quality clothier and his shoes were highly polished. Under his right arm he held a violin case. Indiana assumed the man had come to sell a violin.

"Mr. Jones?" the man asked in a deep voice that sounded as though it had once been far more powerful.

Indiana invited the visitor into the RV.

"My name is Michail Grossman." He looked at Kimberly and said to her, "I was at your performance. You lifted my heart. Such talent for one so young."

"Thank you."

"I read in the newspaper about your plight. So, senseless." He sat on the small couch that faced the dining table. Carefully, he placed the violin case beside him. His gnarled and twisted fingers became obvious to both Indiana and Kimberly. He cleared his throat and asked, "Your violin, Guarneri-style?"

"Yes," Kimberly said offering a sad smile.

"Andrea Guarneri apprenticed alongside Antonio Stradivari in the Amati music workshop in Italy. He then went on to design a violin that I believe has more heart." He turned to the violin case and with difficulty opened the latches. When the top was raised a well-worn soft wine-colored interior was revealed. Nestled in the soft material was a Guarneri-style violin. Michail Grossman sat in silence for a moment looking at the musical instrument. Finally, he lifted it from the case and held it in unsure hands. Slowly, he brought it to his chest and cradled it as a mother would cradle an infant. "I was concert master with the symphony," he reminisced. "The sounds that I was able to get out of this instrument surpassed my talent."

Kimberly looked at the aging musician and understood the pain that he was feeling. After a lifetime of playing he no longer could create music with the violin that he loved. She knew her situation was temporary but Michail Grossman's was not. For him, the music had stopped. He wasn't turning the page he had closed the book.

Michail Grossman continued, "I no longer can play with my arthritis. Even when I did play I couldn't do so with the depth of emotion that you possess. Please, give my violin back its life." Ever so slowly, he removed the violin from his caress and held it out for Kimberly.

Kimberly stood and accepted the instrument. It had signs of wear but also signs of meticulous care. She looked at the open violin case beside the musician and asked, "May I?" He nodded. Kimberly placed the violin on the table. She then removed a bow from the case and tightened the hair. After running the bow across rosin she picked up the violin. She drew the bow across the A string and a beautiful, full, pure sound filled the RV. How long it had been since the violin was played Kimberly didn't know but it was very nearly in-tune. She looked across the neck of the instrument at Michail Grossman whose face seemed brighter and his eyes were fixed on her or the violin. She couldn't really tell. At that moment, having gone without playing for two days and wanting to do something for Mr. Grossman, Kimberly closed her eyes and let her heart speak. Emotions held at bay were released and the small RV was filled with music. For twenty minutes a neglected and hungry violin once more found its voice.

At the conclusion of her impromptu performance Michail Grossman stood and applauded softly with hands wracked in pain. "I have made a wise choice," he said.

"Mr. Grossman," Indiana interjected, "Are you here to sell this violin?"

Michail spoke to Kimberly, "There is a theory that what makes Stradivarius violins so wonderful is the wood that was used. In the period of time between 1645 and 1750 temperatures throughout Europe were far colder than normal. It slowed the growth of trees resulting in unusually dense wood. This instrument was made with maple from the forests of northern Croatia where harsh winters have the same effect. Look at the lines. The wood was then stored in saltwater which caused the pores to close making it even denser. Nicolò Paganini commissioned a luthier to make this Guarneri-style violin in 1839. He died before it was completed. It changed hands a number of times and came into my possession after World War II when the family of a Jewish violinist who died during the war auctioned it off. I was fortunate to have the resources and credit to make such a purchase."

"Mr. Grossman," Indiana once more spoke, "I'm afraid we don't have the resources or credit to make such a purchase."

Still speaking to Kimberly, Michail said, "Without its voice this is only a piece of wood. I can no longer give it its voice, but you can. Please, give it back its soul." He slid the instrument toward Kimberly.

"We simply can't afford it," Indiana insisted.

Finally, Michail Grossman spoke to Indiana, "We have not discussed price, as yet."

"For an instrument such as this, there is no way we have the means to buy it."

"I don't intend to sell it," Michail replied. "I wish to place it in the young lady's care. Something as precious as this should not be owned—it should be played. This I cannot do anymore. I have been trying to decide to whom it should go. When I attended her concert I had my answer."

Both Kimberly and Indiana remained silent not knowing what to say.

Michail Grossman continued, "I do have a few conditions."

Indiana knew there would be conditions.

"I would like to hear this instrument from time to time. So, if possible, I would ask that you perform two concerts a year here in this city. Also, if you would consider sending me a recording of you playing once in a while that would be nice. Finally, when you cannot or choose not to play any longer that you pass this instrument on to the most promising musician that you can find with the same conditions. This way its voice will continue forever."

Kimberly reached out and took the old man's twisted hand and said, "I only hope that I can show this instrument the love that you have and hope that I have sufficient talent to make its voice sing."

Michail Grossman replied, "I am confident that you will." The old man stood and closed the violin case. He stared at its worn surface and patted it gently. "It's funny, unlike us, a piece of maple that weathered terrible cold winters and died is able to produce music and will live forever." He left the RV.

CHAPTER 15

The Black Ice Tour continued. Alicia cried when she heard the story about Michail Grossman surrendering his most precious possession. Yet, she also knew that Kimberly would give that violin a very special voice. While they talked she could hear Kimberly playing in the background. Something struck her about the sound but she wasn't sure what it was.

Their next destination was a small town with a large military base. Alicia had made arrangements for Kimberly to perform on the base from the reviewing stand on the parade ground. The commanding officer, General Randolph Humphries, was skeptical, at first. He wasn't sure that violin music would be much of a draw for an audience. When he heard the performance would be free with donations accepted to support the Wounded Warriors Foundation he agreed.

On the way to the military base Indiana drove in silence. Kimberly sat beside him also in silence. The highway had light traffic and it was a clear sunny day. They passed trees and fields and signs and numerous exits. Both riders were lost in their own thoughts.

Kimberly broke the silence when she said softly, "I'm afraid of the dark."

"You are?" her father replied.

"Don't you remember I always had a nightlight?"

"I thought that was so you could go to the bathroom without bumping into anything."

"That was the cover story."

"Oh."

"Mom knew. I can't stand being in the dark. It scares me."

"I see."

"I don't know what I will do when the permanent darkness comes."

"You don't have to worry about that now," was the only thing Indiana could think of saying.

"But I do. It's going to happen and I dread it. I'll be lost in blackness. It will be terrifying. I'll go mad."

For a moment Indiana wished that Alicia was there. She would know what to say. He was only a truck driver. He didn't know how to talk with a young girl to give her reassurance or hope. It was another case of his daughter needing help and he being incapable of providing it. He took the next exit and drove to a gas station where they could park. When they stopped he looked at Kimberly who was staring straight out the front window of the RV.

"What is it about the dark that scares you?" he asked.

"The dark."

"Are you afraid of something in the dark?"

"You don't understand," Kimberly said with a tone of frustration. "There is nothing in the dark. Nothing. It is empty."

"But, then there shouldn't be anything to fear."

"Dad, you just don't get it."

Indiana didn't know what to say or ask. He could understand being afraid of monsters in the dark or hidden hazards that might hurt you or tripping over something. But, nothing—that poses no threat.

Kimberly tried to explain once more, "Think of how it feels to be falling. It's scary. Total panic until you land. In the dark that's the feeling—only you never land. Just endless panic and fear." A tear ran down her cheek as she added, "And, that's what is going to happen to me!"

Indiana reached over and brought his daughter into his

arms. Indeed, he could understand the fear of falling. But, how was he going to help his daughter turn on a light in the blackness of her mind. It was another case of wanting to fix something that might not be fixable. He tried. "Kim, we all have things that we fear. I'm afraid of heights. That's why I understand the terror that is experienced when falling. I've never actually fallen from a great height but it still is a real fear."

"But, you're not facing being taken to a great height and left there for the rest of your life."

"No, I'm not," Indiana agreed. "However, now that I know you have this fear maybe together we can find a way to alleviate it."

"How?"

"Right now, I don't know," Indiana admitted. "But, I'm confident that together we can beat it."

Father and daughter continued to talk, maybe for the first time. They spent the afternoon sharing feelings, thoughts, concerns, hopes, and dreams. By late afternoon a new bond had developed between them bringing with it a level of trust and affection that both valued. There were lighthearted moments when they both laughed and tender instances, as well.

They arrived at the military base mid-morning the next day. It was the day of the scheduled concert. At the gate they told the guard who they were and why they were there. He replied, "Oh, yeah, the kid with the violin."

The Officer of The Day, Captain Gorman, welcomed Indiana and Kimberly and took them on a tour of the base. In a Humvee they passed barracks, classrooms, on-base family housing, the obstacle course, motor pool, various other training facilities, and the rifle range. They stopped.

A group of young recruits were firing at targets that were twenty yards downrange. Some did well and some were a danger to the cows in the next county. Captain Gorman asked Kimberly if she had ever fired a weapon. When she told him that she hadn't he made a call on his radio then said, "I have clearance to let you take a few shots." He turned to Indiana and added, "With your permission, sir."

Training was paused and all weapons secured. All the recruits then watched as Kimberly was given instructions by a burly sergeant on how to fire an M-16. From a prone position Kimberly took aim. She pulled the trigger and it fired. The recoil wasn't as great as she had expected. An indicator lit the position where she hit the target. It was just outside the bull's-eye to the right. "Holy crap!" one recruit said. The sergeant knelt down and told Kimberly, "This time don't pull the trigger because it moves the rifle slightly to the right." Then he said something that surprised all who could hear, "Think of pushing down on the E string of your violin." Kimberly did as instructed and her next four rounds hit the bull's-eye which drew applause from the onlookers.

"Thank you so much," Kimberly said to the sergeant, "That was exciting. Do you play the violin?"

The sergeant looked around sheepishly, "I play some. Not like I heard you can play."

"Would you play for me?"

"Listen, kid, it's not the kind of thing that someone in my position does."

"Please."

"I can't, sorry."

"If you change your mind," Kimberly pouted, "we have an RV over there somewhere."

"Thanks, but no."

"I hope you come to the concert tonight."

The sergeant replied, "I'll be there in the front row."

After lunch they returned to Mozart, the Ford RV. The

rest of the day was their time until the concert. In mid-afternoon there was a knock on the RV door. Kimberly opened the door, smiled, and said, "I knew you would come."

"Yeah, well I didn't," Sergeant Vincent Webb replied. He carried a violin case and kept looking around hoping that no one would see him.

Inside the RV Kimberly and Sergeant Webb talked about music. He had studied violin before joining the military. Whenever he had opportunities off-base he would play simple tunes and attempt more complex pieces. He and Kimberly each played for each other and gave meaning to music being the universal language. After one particular piece, Kimberly asked Sergeant Webb if he would play it at the concert.

"Are you crazy!" He protested, "I'd never live it down. Kid, I intimidate these recruits and push them to do things they never thought they could."

"Sergeant Webb," Kimberly answered, "there's all kinds of courage. You have talent. Do you have the courage to show it?"

"Don't pull that crap on me. I do it every day. I'm an expert at motivation."

Kimberly continued, "Yet, you hide something you love."

"It doesn't fit this situation."

"Just play one piece—that one—I'll play with you."

"Out of the question."

"Sergeant," Indiana chimed in, "she has a way of making things happen."

"Not this time," the tougher-than-nails non-com stood, thanked Kimberly, and left. His violin remained on the couch.

When the time for the concert arrived there were

approximately eighty people in the audience. As promised, Sergeant Webb sat in the front row. A number of officers were in attendance with their wives. Kimberly walked up onto the reviewing stand wearing a full-length blue dress. Her hair was pulled back into a ponytail. To start things off with energy and excitement she played *The Storm*, from Vivaldi's *Four Seasons*. It was followed by a lively *The Fairy Fiddler* from *Symphony No. 2* by John Joubert. She finished the first half of the program with *Symphony No. 5* by Beethoven.

After the intermission Kimberly started off with the energetic *Riverdance*. She then switched to a contemporary piece, *Hijo de la Luna,* which means *Son of The Moon.* Written by José María Cano for the band Mecano in 1986, its haunting melody combined melancholy with hope. As the song progresses it grows in strength with dramatic tones and phrases then fades into a soft end. Kimberly then walked over to the microphone and said, "This next piece was composed by Giuseppe Tartini who was an Italian Baroque composer and violinist. Tartini was the first known owner of a violin made by Antonio Stradivari in 1715. His *Violin Sonata in G Minor* is titled *The Devil's Trill.* There is a story that goes with it." She unfolded a piece of paper and read.

"One night, in the year 1713 I dreamed I had made a pact with the devil for my soul. Everything went as I wished: my new servant anticipated my every desire. Among other things, I gave him my violin to see if he could play. How great was my astonishment on hearing a sonata so wonderful and so beautiful, played with such great art and intelligence, as I had never even conceived in my boldest flights of fantasy. I felt enraptured, transported, enchanted: my breath failed me, and - I awoke. I immediately grasped my violin in order to retain, in part at least, the impression of my dream. In vain! The music which I at this time composed is indeed the best that I ever wrote, and I still call it the "Devil's Trill", but the difference between it and that which so moved me is so great that I would have destroyed my instrument and have said farewell to music forever if it had been possible for me to live without the enjoyment it affords me."

"No one should have to live without music," Kimberly said as she looked at Sergeant Webb. She brought her violin up to her chin and began. Tones and notes spoke directly to the big soldier. The sounds combined strength with tenderness. Sadness was drawn from within the man. Yet, higher tones uplifted him. An abrupt change in tempo brought forth the excitement of youth of innocence of hope and the fulfillment of dreams. Sergeant Webb watched a young girl's hands glide across strings and the bow play upon them. Their eyes met and Kimberly winked. Once more the music changed as if pleading. Then more energy, anguish, lighthearted dancing, ascending runs, a cry of desperation, lively patter, high pitched exclamations, calming tones, and a final slow dissolve into silence.

After the applause Kimberly returned to the microphone. It was then that she noticed that the audience had grown to well over a hundred. She said in a soft voice, "I shot a rifle today." This brought cheers and applause. Kimberly continued, "It was thrilling. To hold that much power in my hands. It also scared me. I met a soldier today who is a master marksman who also has musical talent. He holds two kinds of power in his hands. I'd like to invite him to play a duet with me. I won't name him and if he refuses I understand. But, remember music has a power all its own. This last piece was my heartfelt request for his presence on the stage. I can say no more." Kimberly walked over to the side of the reviewing stand where Indiana was and retrieved Sergeant Webb's violin. She held it over her head and said, "Locked and loaded!"

The audience exploded with applause and a chant began, "Join her. Join her. Join her." Finally, Sergeant Vincent Webb stood. His imposing size made it impossible to miss him. The applause increased peppered with a few whistles. He strode up onto the reviewing stand and said in a low voice, "Combat was easier than this." He took his violin and added, "Your father was right."

"He usually is," Kimberly replied, "You start and I'll join you. Play until I signal to stop."

Sergeant Vincent Webb turned to face the audience. He felt weak in the knees and his hands shook. The image of the huge sergeant in camo next to a small twelve-year-old girl in a long blue dress was striking. His size made his violin appear small. After taking a breath he began. The pure and full notes he played were joined by Kimberly's as together they played the song *Danny Boy*. The crowd fell silent. When he began the second stanza, Kimberly stepped back and played a softer background interpretation. Then in the third stanza she began to play flourishes and improvised enhancements. This caused Sergeant Webb to also take liberties with the music. They turned to face each other and began a kind of dueling violins. Somewhere in the audience a harmonica joined them. Then a tenor voice was heard in the back singing the lyrics of *Danny Boy*. The whole performance took on a life of its own. The magic continued through a fourth stanza when Kimberly smiled and nodded and they ended with a flourish.

Sergeant Webb and a young girl who was afraid of the dark held hands and accepted the gratitude of the crowd. He turned to Kimberly and smiled.

"Another river crossed," Kimberly said.

CHAPTER 16

A banging came to the RV door. It was the morning after the concert at the military base. Indiana and Kimberly had remained on the base overnight with plans to leave mid-day. The thumping on the door awakened them. Indiana looked around and found his watch. It was 5:30 a.m. Once more thumping demanded to be answered. Finally, Indiana made his way to the door and opened it. Before him stood the imposing figure of Sergeant Vincent Webb.

"Saddle-up! You're about to miss breakfast!" the drill instructor stated.

"Breakfast?"

"The young lady is in demand."

"Oh, by whom?"

"After word about last night spread those who didn't attend expressed disappointment."

"I'm sorry to hear that, but we're leaving today," Indiana explained.

"The request comes from General Humphries," Sergeant Webb said with a tone of resignation.

"He was at the concert. I saw him," Kimberly said as she entered the sitting area of the RV.

"He was, indeed, young lady."

"I hope he enjoyed my, uh, our performance," she said with a smile.

"That he did," Sergeant Webb replied. "He would like you, me, and your father to join him at his residence for breakfast."

"I take it that was more than a request," Indiana concluded.

"When a general makes a request it is always an order,"

the sergeant stated.

At precisely 6:00 a.m. the three arrived at General Randolph Humphries' residence. They were ushered into the dining room where they joined General Humphries and his wife Lillian.

"That was quite a performance last night, Miss Jones," the general stated over a cup of black coffee.

"Thank you."

"Yes, it was quite remarkable," he continued. "All in attendance were very impressed. Lillian and I enjoyed every minute of the event. In fact, my adjutant received numerous requests from officers and non-commissioned officers, who missed last night, for a repeat performance."

"We plan to leave today," Indiana said.

"Yes?" the general stared directly at Indiana.

"We, uh, have to get to the next destination on our tour."

"And, where is that?"

"Well, we don't know."

"Oh."

"Yes. We are told on Monday where we need to be on Thursday by our manager who sets up the concerts."

"I see. Then it is not essential that you leave today," General Humphries raised his chin slightly and looked out of the bottom of his eyes at Indiana.

"Well, no."

"Then I would appreciate it as a personal favor if you," he looked in the direction of Sergeant Webb, "and Sergeant Webb would give us the honor of performing a second concert tonight."

"I don't play for free," Kimberly said to everyone's surprise.

"Understood," the general said without missing a beat. "Tell me your fee and I'll have my adjutant make arrangements for payment."

"Not money," Kimberly said. "I've never been on an Army base before. I'd like to see more of it and meet the soldiers. Something for me to take away in my memory is worth far more than money."

General Humphries smiled, "Very good. You will have the full visiting Senator treatment."

"My dear," Lillian Humphries said, "You play so beautifully. I enjoyed every minute last night. Would you join me and some officers' wives for lunch?" Her smile was genuine but had a shadow of sadness that did not escape Kimberly.

"I would be glad to," Kimberly said.

After breakfast things happened fast. A First Lieutenant was assigned to give Indiana and Kimberly a tour of the base. Their first stop was the parade ground where close order drills and inspections were being executed. Then they visited barracks, the mess hall, classrooms, and on-base housing. They passed the rifle range with which Kimberly was familiar and continued on to an area where a number of M1A2 Abrams tanks were being prepped.

"The M1A2 Abrams tank is named after General Creighton Abrams, former Army Chief of Staff and Commander of U.S. military forces in the Vietnam War from 1968 to 1972," the Lieutenant stated. "It weighs almost 62 tons and features a powerful gas turbine engine, composite armor, and sophisticated electronics. The main gun is a 105mm L7."

They approached one of the huge vehicles which became more and more imposing the closer they came. Kimberly put her hand on the tank, turned toward Indiana, and said, "Now, this is something I'd like to drive."

"That would be impossible," the Lieutenant stated. "It

takes a great deal of training to drive one of these, not to mention clearance needed."

As they started to walk away a Captain came around the tank. He immediately recognized Kimberly and said in a booming voice, "Hey, you're the little girl with the violin."

The tour group stopped.

"I never thought I would like that long-hair music but you changed my mind. What was that song you talked about before playing?"

"*The Devil's Trill* by Giuseppe Tartini," Kimberly answered with a smile.

"Yeah? I gotta get me a copy of that." He patted the tank and asked, "Have you seen my devil?"

"It's quite impressive. I wish I could drive it," Kimberly said.

"I told her that was impossible, sir," the Lieutenant stated.

The Captain rubbed his chin as he thought. "Now, that's not exactly correct. If we had proper clearance . . ." He walked over to the tank and made a call on his cellphone. The group couldn't hear what he was saying but his laughter gave the impression that the conversation was going well. When he returned to the group he stated, "Well Senator, the Company Commander said at my discretion." He looked at Kimberly critically and said, "You look too young to drive."

"She can drive a Kenworth T700 tractor with 40 foot trailer," Indiana said with pride as he placed his hand on Kimberly's shoulder.

"Yeah? Double clutch?"

"Better than me."

"OK then, let's get this baby moving." The Captain climbed onto the tank, reached down, and pulled Kimberly aboard. He looked over at Indiana and said, "Come'on dad—unless you're afraid."

In an instant Indiana was on the tank. For the next hour Kimberly was instructed on how to drive the M1A2 Abrams. Due to sophisticated electronics the 62 ton vehicle was easier to drive than one would think. They proceeded down a tank trail that crossed a spring went up a steep incline and entered a large field. There Kimberly was allowed to open her up and see how fast the big imposing war machine could travel. At 32 miles-per-hour the feeling that came with handling so much power was overwhelming and Kimberly laughed. Indiana sat in the loader's seat that was above and behind the driver and below the tank commander. Because they all wore headphones he could hear Kimberly and smiled when he heard her laugh. In his heart he wanted her to experience as much as she could and enjoy all the magic of life. Unfortunately, in the back of his mind he couldn't help but face the unbearable fact that her ability to do these things was limited by an unknown length of time.

The final stop in the morning was a small museum and library on the base. It was filled with various displays of historical battles and equipment. Rows of books on military history and strategy filled a large portion of the room. Kimberly explored looking at the various military artifacts until she found in one corner a table with a small display. It had a picture of a soldier who had paid the ultimate price in battle. A young man in uniform with a serious look on his face stood proudly before them. On the table were medals the fallen soldier had been awarded. A sword in its scabbard lay across the table. The name of the soldier was Captain Daniel Humphries.

At lunch with the officers' wives Kimberly asked Lillian Humphries about the display.

"He was our son," she replied sadly.

"I'm sorry," Kimberly said.

"We are a military family, dear. We live with a sword dangling above our heads never knowing when it might fall," she explained. "Daniel was proud to be a soldier. He was a model soldier and doing what he wanted most to do. We supported his choice. We . . . were . . . very proud . . . of him." She sipped some wine and added softly, "I miss him."

Kimberly asked, "Mrs. Humphries is there anything that I can play tonight as a tribute to your son?"

"You already did," she replied, "last night, you and Sergeant Webb."

The rest of the day was spent touring the base and meeting soldiers. Those who had attended the last evening's performance were excited to meet Kimberly. A few asked for her autograph. Many said they were planning to attend the Friday night concert.

When concert time arrived the audience was standing room only. Kimberly walked onto the reviewing platform wearing long black wide-leg pants and a light blue silk blouse. She walked up to the microphone and said, "I drove a tank, today."

The audience cheered with a distinct, "Who Rah!"

"I also met so many wonderful people who are serving our country that it made me feel very small. You handle so much awesome responsibility and work so hard to be good at what you do. And, all I have is a violin. I'll do my best not to make it fubar," she said using a term she learned during the day which means; fouled up beyond all recognition or a variation thereof. The audience laughed and some whistles were heard.

Kimberly repeated the previous evening's performance with a few changes and additions. She played *Pavane for a Dead Princess* by French composer Maurice Ravel. As she did she looked at her father as it was his favorite piece. For a few moments they were alone sharing thoughts filled with love. *The Devil's Trill* was played for Captain Inwan. Earlier in the day Kimberly recorded a version of the piece and left it for the Captain. In addition, she also added the *Flight of The Bumblebee* as a crowd pleaser. As with the night before, she invited Sergeant Webb to join her for the final piece. This time he didn't protest. When he joined her on stage she whispered to him, "After the second repeat don't listen to me." He nodded and they began playing *Danny Boy* together. When Sergeant Webb began playing the melody for the third time Kimberly played *God Bless America* in the background at the same tempo. The effect was powerful causing the audience to sit in silence. When they finished, for a brief moment, not a sound was heard on the parade ground. Applause then filled the air.

After the concert General Humphries and his wife stopped Indiana and Kimberly. "Once again, a brilliant performance," the camp commander stated.

"It was lovely, dear," Lillian Humphries said. She took Kimberly's hands and said softly, "A perfect tribute. Thank you."

"I wish I could have done more," Kimberly responded.

General Humphries then said, "I have one more favor to ask. It's not what you think. Join us for breakfast tomorrow and I'll explain." He smiled, as did Lillian, and they left.

CHAPTER 17

Once again Indiana and Kimberly found themselves at the dining room table having breakfast with General Humphries and his wife. This time the atmosphere was more friendly and familiar. General Humphries was quite complimentary of the performance and added, "Lillian and I were quite touched by your tribute to our son, Daniel."

"The night before was enough, but what you played last night was so very special," his wife added.

"The performance was videotaped," the General stated. "We will make sure that you receive a special copy before you leave." He then in a lighter tone asked, "Did you enjoy your tour of the base?"

"Very much," Kimberly answered. "But it did make me sad. I wanted to meet the soldiers, but when I did I couldn't help wondering if they would be hurt or killed in the near future. It was like a thousand good-byes."

Silence hung over the room. The clink of silverware on plates seemed louder than usual. Each diner drifted into private thoughts and faced a reality that normally goes unspoken. Finally, General Humphries changed the mood when he said, "I told you I have another favor to ask which is why I invited you to breakfast, once more." He took a sip of coffee and explained, "You, of course, can refuse but I don't think that will happen." Kimberly looked at her father and then back at the General. He continued, "The military is a large family and contrary to appearances each branch of service does not operate completely separate from the others. In fact, many senior officers interact with senior officers of other branches on a regular basis." He addressed his next comments directly to Kimberly. "You are a very talented young lady. We have been pleasantly surprised by your performances and the reaction of our personnel. I made reference to this in a recent conversation with Admiral Blatnicky. He commands CSG 66 which is a carrier strike group." When he observed the blank stares from his guests he explained, "A carrier strike group is made up of an aircraft carrier and support craft such as guided missile cruisers, destroyers, LAMPS, submarines, and other defensive or support craft."

A member of the staff entered the room and removed dishes from the table. The General continued, "CSG 66 is off the coast at this moment executing final trials before being deployed. Admiral Blatnicky and I are longtime friends." General Humphries looked at his wife and said with a smile, "His wife introduced Lillian and me." He returned his attention to Kimberly, "He would like me to invite you to perform on the aircraft carrier in his strike group."

"When?" Indiana asked.

"Tonight."

"Tonight? How would we get there?"

"If you agree to perform a helicopter will be sent to take you to the ship."

"I don't perform for free," Kimberly stated.

This time the General was not caught off guard. He looked directly at the twelve-year-old girl and asked, "And, what is your fee this time?"

"I want to ride in a jet."

The General did not expect that request and his facial expression revealed his surprise. It was a rare event for General Humphries to show a reaction. Kimberly smiled.

"Now, Kimberly, that is out of the question," Indiana said across the table. "It's dangerous and they would never allow it."

Kimberly looked at her father and said, "We are on a quest for me to see all that I can before it becomes impossible. I'm not afraid." She then turned toward General Humphries and said, "You're a General." He nodded. "You can do anything."

General Humphries chuckled and replied, "We Generals like to think we can do anything, but that's not the case. Authorizing a civilian on a fighter aircraft not only would have to be approved by the Admiral, but also the Captain of the ship, Flight Wing Commander, Squadron Commander, and the pilot. It's very unlikely that it could happen."

"Then it's very unlikely that I will play," Kimberly responded in a firm no-nonsense voice.

"Captain Ritter," the General called out. When his aide entered the room he ordered, "Relay to Admiral Blatnicky Miss Kimberly Jones requirement of a jet ride as compensation for her performing tonight."

"A jet ride?" the surprised officer stated.

"You'll get her a jet ride or you'll be taking a ride to the Aleutians," the General snapped.

"Yes sir," the officer quickly left the room.

"Now, that officer's future is in your hands," General Humphries informed Kimberly. "If he fails in his assignment his next assignment will be in a faraway base counting spent cartridges."

"I didn't mean . . ." Kimberly began a look of concern upon her face.

General Humphries laughed, "Don't try to feed me a soup sandwich, young lady. I know when I'm being yahooed."

"Then he won't get in trouble?" Kimberly asked still not quite sure what to think.

"Captain Ritter? Fine officer. I couldn't get along without him."

Kimberly relented and asked, "Good. What time do we leave for the boat?"

"Ship," General Humphries corrected, "We'll let you know as soon as arrangements have been made."

A Seahawk SH-60 helicopter arrived at the army base at 1100 hours. Kimberly and her father were waiting with overnight bags. These aircraft are used for combat missions, search and rescue, supply replenishment, and other tasks. Its sleek profile and weapons pods gave it a true combat military appearance. An Ensign walked over to the waiting pair. "Sir, Miss, I'm Ensign Triplett. If you are ready we can proceed to the carrier." He took their bags but Kimberly wouldn't let him take her violin case.

Indiana climbed aboard the waiting helicopter while Ensign Triplett helped Kimberly get on board. Inside the small cabin there were three seats against the rear bulkhead approximately three feet from the large open sliding door. The sliding door on the opposite side of the aircraft was closed. A seat was bolted to the floor next to the large window in the far side door. Ensign Triplett motioned for Kimberly to take that seat. "It provides the best view."

Indiana sat in the middle seat to the rear of the aircraft.

"I'm going to keep this door open for better air circulation," the Ensign said, "So strap yourselves in." He sat in the open doorway with his legs dangling outside.

Kimberly looked at her father with a huge grin. What she saw was a man who was visibly uncomfortable with the whole experience. It was then that she remembered him telling her of his fear of heights. He was obviously not happy and they hadn't even left the ground. When he saw her looking he forced a half-smile and gave her a thumbs-up. She turned toward the front of the helicopter and could see the two pilots preparing for flight. Then the big rotor increased rotation and they abruptly lifted off. Behind her she heard her father say, "Oh boy!"

The SH-60 helicopter tilted and rapidly moved forward. Its power and speed was thrilling to at least one passenger. It was terrorizing to the other. Below was the vast army base which dropped farther and farther away and finally slid behind and out of sight. After a twenty minute flight they were over water. Noise inside the cabin was overwhelming making any conversation nearly impossible. Kimberly concluded that combat aircraft were not designed to provide creature comfort. The view however was spectacular. She tried to will a memory of what she saw.

Landing a helicopter on the rising and falling deck of an aircraft carrier is not as easy as one might think. It's a matter of physics and timing. They approach the carrier from the side matching its forward speed. Then slowly the aircraft moves over the deck where an interesting, and unexpected by Indiana and Kimberly, effect takes place. When the downdraft of the large rotor goes from over water to over a solid and much closer deck the aircraft abruptly rises. Seasoned sailors and pilots know this but Indiana didn't which was why he exclaimed, "Holy Crap!"

Touchdown is also referred to as a controlled crash. The pilot watches a green-shirted helicopter landing signal enlisted sailor (LSE) who indicates the changing distance from the deck. Good shock absorbers and slow descent bring the craft and carrier together with a noticeable thud.

"That was fun," Kimberly acknowledged as she turned to look at her father who simple nodded.

The XO, Executive Officer, greeted the pair at the SH-60, "Welcome aboard. I'm Commander Chen. I'll take you to your quarters and then to meet the Captain." He looked at his watch, "You made good time." A wobbly Indiana and energized Kimberly followed the officer.

Captain Joseph Ballantine met with Indiana and Kimberly in a squadron ready room. The tall, fit, sun-tanned officer had all the features you would expect from the person in command of such a large and powerful ship. His demeanor matched his appearance. As a result, when Indiana shook his hand he said, "Pleasure to meet you, sir." It was probably the first time he used the term "sir" since he was a teenager. Kimberly was speechless.

"We are looking forward to your concert this evening," Captain Ballantine said to Kimberly, who nodded. "However, I believe at the moment we have something more important to address." Out of the shadows another officer appeared. "This is Lieutenant JG O'Rourke. He is a pilot and will be briefing you." Kimberly looked at the pilot and was a bit confused.

"How are you Kimberly," Lieutenant O'Rourke said as he took her hand.

Kimberly looked at her father, the Captain, and back to the pilot, "Uh, I'm fine, I guess."

"Good."

Captain Ballantine stated, "Lieutenant O'Rourke has volunteered to take you up." He paused, "If that is still your desire." The commanding officer walked to the door, turned back, and said, "This is very atypical and not directly covered by regulations. Someone with a lot of juice pulled the right strings." His gaze was directed at Kimberly, "The decision was made above my pay grade. Someone out there likes you." The Captain disappeared into a corridor.

Lieutenant O'Rourke picked up the conversation, "You will have to be examined by the flight surgeon, receive protocol training, and be fitted with a flight suit."

"OK," was all Kimberly could mutter.

"As her father, we need your authorization," Lieutenant O'Rourke told Indiana.

"I don't know," Indiana started, "It's very dangerous . . ."

"I'll be fine, dad," Kimberly said in a pleading tone.

With all the necessary steps taken, Kimberly Jones found herself in the rear seat of an EA-18G Growler jet aircraft. She was wearing a flight suit and helmet. Two sailors that strapped her in reminded her of the location of the eject lever. Lieutenant O'Rourke sat in front. He finished his preflight check list and closed the canopy. Kimberly was afraid but also fascinated. Sailors in different color shirts scurried around the deck attending to their specialized duties, the drone of the jet engines drowned out most other sounds, Lieutenant O'Rourke's voice echoed in her earphones as he communicated with flight command, and her heartbeat pounded in her head. The unarmed aircraft was positioned on the deck at the end of the catapult. A tow bar was attached to the nose gear and also to the catapult shuttle. Behind the plane the jet blast deflector (jbd) was raised. The Catapult Control Officer then monitored buildup of pressure in two long pistons under the deck. When the appropriate steam pressure for the jet to take off was reached he signaled the pilot. At this point Lieutenant O'Rourke said to Kimberly, "Lean back in your seat," and brought the twin engines up to takeoff thrust. In a few seconds the Catapult Control Officer released the pistons and the catapult thrust the aircraft forward from 0 to 165 miles-per-hour in two seconds.

"Holy shit!" Kimberly exclaimed as the jet went skyward.

"That about sums it up," O'Rourke replied.

"It took my breath away."

"How are you feeling?"

"Scared, a little woozy, but wow! It's amazing. I can't believe that I'm actually here."

"I'm going to make a few easy turns so you won't feel too many G's."

"You must love doing this," Kimberly concluded.

"I do," Lieutenant O'Rourke admitted. He then said, "I volunteered for this flight."

"Thank you."

"I volunteered because I have a twelve-year-old daughter at home. I miss her. I'm away too long on deployments. In an odd funny kind of way it's like you are a stand-in for my daughter. It's like having her along seeing what her dad does every day."

"Well, I hope she wouldn't say what I did."

"Even that would be music to my ears."

"What's her name?"

"Judith, uh Judy."

"She must be very proud of you."

"I really don't know."

The rest of the flight was routine for Lieutenant O'Rourke but a thrill ride for Kimberly. She told the Navy pilot how proud she was of her father and that she never tells him. "It's just the way we twelve-year-olds are," she explained. "In many ways we are more concerned with you being proud of us."

Lieutenant O'Rourke brought the big jet back to the aircraft carrier and put it down perfectly on the deck with the tailhook catching the third wire. This is the wire they aim for when landing. He went to full power until he felt the arresting wire pulling back on the aircraft. Once out of the plane and on the deck Kimberly thanked Lieutenant O'Rourke, ran over to Indiana and told him how proud she was to have him as her dad.

The concert Kimberly did that evening was filled with energized pieces, patriotic songs, and the Navy Hymn. She ended the concert by saying, "I know this is being taped. So, I want Judy O'Rourke to know how proud your father is of you and that this original composition is dedicated to you." Kimberly closed her eyes and began to play.

CHAPTER 18

With their military experience behind them, Indiana and Kimberly were once more on the road. Kimberly was listening to Alicia on her smart phone. She wrote down the name of the next destination and got directions. At one point she laughed and said, "Oh, he's going to love it." Kimberly then asked, "Do you want to speak with him?" After a pause she stated, "You're afraid aren't you?" A short time later the phone call ended.

Indiana having listened to one half of the conversation asked, "OK, where to and why am I going to love it. Or, more accurately not be thrilled by it?"

"Well, it's not exactly what we are used to."

"OK, come clean. Spill it. Confess," Indiana said.

"Good choice of words," Kimberly concluded, "it's a penitentiary."

"A what!"

"A prison."

"Is Alicia out of her mind?" Indiana bellowed, quickly found a gas station, and pulled off the road. He took the phone from Kimberly and pressed the speed dial button for Shaun and Alicia Harper. After five rings Shaun answered the phone.

"I know Alicia is there," Indiana said in a stern tone, "I must speak to her."

"Indiana, I realize this sounds outrageous . . ." Shaun began.

"You think?"

"But, wait, there is a story that goes with it."

"There is nothing that can be said that makes sending a twelve-year-old girl to a prison a good idea!"

"It's not a maximum security prison."

"That puts my mind at ease—how?"

"It's a new concept aimed at turning first offenders around before it's too late."

"That's nice but it's not a nice place for my daughter."

"They are trying to use different technique to motivate inmates to follow a better path. Music is one approach."

"Good—play CDs."

"They have invested in musical instruments but haven't generated any interest."

"So, bringing in a twelve-year-old girl is their answer? No way! Forget it!"

"The Warden read about the Black Ice tour and contacted us. He also called in some favors and has the local Lion's Club as the sponsor. They are raising money to pay for the performance."

"All that is very nice, but it doesn't change my opinion. My daughter is not going into a dangerous situation."

"I rode in a jet," Kimberly said hearing Indiana's position.

Indiana looked at his daughter. He responded, "That's different. These are criminals."

"It's just another experience," she said, "Honestly, I'd be more comfortable there than in a school."

Kimberly's statement brought Indiana back to the loss of her violin and her outburst about hating school. She carried a great deal of pain from her experience with the educational system. However, Indiana wondered if it was wise to introduce her to the penal system? It could prove to be yet another source of pain. And, it was pain that he was trying so hard to protect her from. The possibilities were so unpredictable. It was like taking her into a dark cave without knowing what was inside. As a father he knew that would be irresponsible. Far better that she be angry for a short period than scarred for life.

"Let's do it," Kimberly finally said with a smile.

"We don't know what we are getting into," was her father's response.

"It will be an adventure," Kimberly argued, "I won't go in with any great expectations."

"I hope we don't regret it."

The decision made, they drove to the designated prison. The facility was clean and new. It was the modern style of a central common area surrounded by five stories of cells. On one side was the main enclosed control booth with bulletproof glass and tamperproof doors. Opposite this guard post was a corridor that led to dining on the left and an auditorium on the right. The planned performance was scheduled earlier than usual as it would immediately follow dinner when inmates were already out of their cells.

As first offenders most of the inmates were young. Sprinkled among them were some who were middle-aged. They shuffled into the auditorium and slowly took their seats. Guards lined the walls and provided security for the stage. When everyone had settled down the Warden introduced the evening's performer.

Kimberly Jones walked onto the stage carrying her violin. She was dressed quite conservatively wearing slacks and boyish style blouse. Her hair was pulled back in a ponytail.

She began with Ludwig van Beethoven's *Violin Concerto in D major, Op. 61.*

At first there was silence. A few snickers were heard. Then murmurs spread as inmates expressed their displeasure. "What kind of crap is this?" "Jeez, my ears." "Let's hear some real music." As the comments spread laughter followed.

Kimberly stopped playing. She decided that her choice

of music was not appropriate for the audience that sat before her. She changed style and played and Irish folk song, *Toss The Feathers*. The faster tempo and upbeat tone was expected to be better received. It wasn't. A combination of complaints, laughter, and boos from the restless crowd caused the Warden to stop the concert. He angrily instructed the guards to return inmates to their cells. Kimberly left the stage.

Indiana was waiting for Kimberly and comforted her, "I'm sorry, Kim. They're not ready for our kind of music." He made sure that he didn't in any way give the impression that he was saying, "I told you so."

"Not quite the adventure we expected," Kimberly said. She then added in a contemplative manner, "I wonder what is their kind of music?"

"It doesn't matter. We're out of here," her father responded with a hint of anger.

The Warden joined Indiana and Kimberly. He shook his head. "I really thought they would respond better than that." He looked at Kimberly and apologized, "I'm sorry. If I had known I wouldn't have invited you to play. What I did get to hear, I very much enjoyed." He motioned with his arm toward a rear door and stated, "We can go out this way."

"Can I see the prison?" Kimberly asked which surprised both her father and the Warden.

"Do you really want to?" the amazed Warden asked.

"Yes."

"I need to confirm that everyone is in lockdown," he explained. He took a walkie-talkie out of his pocket and inquired as to inmate status. When lockdown was confirmed he led the two visitors into the corridor between the dining area and the auditorium. They were shown the dining area and food preparation area and returned to the corridor. Then they entered the circular common area. It was immense in size with the five stories of cells around the circumference making Indiana and Kimberly feel very small. The Warden described the facility and explained the function of the enclosed guard station. As they walked toward it a lone harmonica was heard emanating from one of the top floors. Kimberly didn't recognize it but the inmate was playing Muddy Water's *I Just Want To Make Love To You*. She stopped.

Indiana and the Warden watched in silence as Kimberly opened her violin case and removed her instrument. After a few moments of listening she began to play along with the far off harmonica. The acoustics in the enormous circular building were excellent. The inmate hearing Kimberly's violin switched to John Sabastian's *Orange Dude Blues*. Kimberly, accustomed as she was with extemporaneous playing, enhanced the harmonica music. In another cell an inmate began drumming on the bars. This was against the rules but the Warden didn't intercede. He stood beside Indiana and watched Kimberly play blues violin with the inmates.

The tone then changed as the inmate played an upbeat jazz piece, *Little Walter's Jump*. Kimberly started tapping her foot and moving around the common area as she played freestyle along with her unknown accompanist. From other cells were heard shouts of approval, "Yeah!" "Do it baby!" "I dig it!" Another drummer joined the group then an inmate imitated a saxophone. The next piece was even more energetic as they began to jam. At one point and unplanned each played a solo. When Kimberly did her part she closed her eyes and played. Her fingers danced upon the strings and her bow flew with rapier speed. The twelve-year-old played with such feeling and enthusiasm inmates in other cells began to clap along or stamp their feet. Before long the entire prison exploded with noise and vibration from inmate involvement.

The Warden stood in disbelief. He looked up at the cells and turned 360 degrees as he considered the phenomenon. It was a happening that was occurring before his very eyes. The Captain of the guards joined the Warden. Neither spoke. They stood looking up at what might have been defined as a riot if it wasn't for the fact that it was a musical jam session.

When they finished the freestyle piece, an inmate yelled out, "Crossroads!" Kimberly didn't know what that meant and she looked at the Warden. From above the harmonica began playing the blues song written by Robert Johnson of San Antonio, Texas in 1936. Kimberly played along and the inmate that requested the song began to sing.

> I went to the crossroad, fell down on my knees
> I went to the crossroad, fell down on my knees
> Asked the lord above "Have mercy, save poor Bob, if you please"
>
> Mmmmm, standin' at the crossroad, I tried to flag a ride
> Standin' at the crossroad, I tried to flag a ride
> Didn't nobody seem to know me, everybody pass me by
>
> Mmmm, the sun goin' down, boy, dark gon' catch me here
> Oooo, eeee, boy, dark gon' catch me here
> I haven't got no lovin' sweet woman that love and feel my care
>
> You can run, you can run, tell my friend-boy Willie Brown
> You can run, tell my friend-boy Willie Brown
> Lord I'm standin' at the crossroad, babe, I believe I'm sinkin' down

The concert, jam session, lasted over an hour. When it ended, a deep voice from above bellowed, "Thank you, little girl." It was followed by applause. Kimberly stood in the middle of the common area surrounded by five floors of cells that housed a faceless audience. Tears streamed down her cheeks. She didn't know if she was crying for herself or for them. Silently she and her father left the common area.

Outside the prison, the Warden thanked them for what they did. He told them that he decided to have a regular Friday night jam session in the auditorium. He was confident that the musical instruments would be put to good use.

CHAPTER 19

Kimberly reached out for her glass. Instead of easily picking it up she hit it and knocked it over. Water flowed across the little table in the Ford RV causing Indiana to jump from his seat.

"I'm sorry," she said, "I don't know how I misjudged it."

"Don't worry, sweetie. It's only water." Indiana grabbed a roll of paper towels and began swabbing up the escaping liquid. When he looked over at Kimberly he noticed that she was repeatedly moving her hand toward the now upright glass. Most often she grasped it normally, however, every once in a while, she hit the glass with her fingertips. Something was wrong and even though he feared the answer he asked, "What's the matter, Kim?"

She didn't answer. Again and again she tested her ability to pick up the glass. Indiana finished cleaning up. Finally, Kimberly looked at her father and answered, "There are times when the glass isn't where I think it is. It's slightly over to the right of where I see it."

"Do you see it clearly with both eyes?" Indiana asked knowing that through triangulation one judges distance.

"No. My left eye sees it clearly but my right eye is cloudy. I see it but not as sharp."

A cold chill passed through Indiana. He knew vision issues would eventually manifest themselves but thought they were still off in a distant future. It was too soon. He said what had to be said, "Maybe, we should see a doctor."

Kimberly looked at her father and without emotion replied, "We know what they'll say. And, there'll be endless tests with the same result and prediction."

Indiana understood her reluctance and wrestled with himself as to what was in his daughter's best interest. There wasn't a definitive answer. On one hand it would involve banks of tests, doctor's conferences, serious facial expressions, and apologetic diagnosis. On the other, they could be ignoring important symptoms of the progression of her disease.

"Dusk," Kimberly said softly.

"What?"

"Dusk comes before the darkness," she said. "We need to continue the Black Ice Tour because we are running out of time."

The telephone rang which ended any further discussion on the subject. Kimberly grabbed it without difficulty. She spoke with Alicia. "I know it turned out great. Yes, in the beginning, I thought I was going to bomb . . . Music is magic. I hope it saves some of those poor souls . . . This week? Friday and Saturday? Well, I've never played with an orchestra . . . Rehearsal? Thursday and Friday? I'm willing to try. I just hope that I don't let them down. Who? OK." She hung up.

"What's our destination?"

"A city youth orchestra wants me to solo."

"That should be fun."

"We have to be there Thursday for rehearsals. The performances are Friday and Saturday." Kimberly sat silently looking out the side window of the RV. She was lost in thought. Indiana let her have time to think. She then stated emphatically, "I hope it's not at a school."

No more was said about her eyesight. On their way to their next destination they visited a number of historical sights, tourist traps, and a quiet forest complete with streams and a waterfall. Lush green surroundings, dueling birds, a chorus of insects, and rushing water offered a welcome escape. Father and daughter enjoyed communing with nature. At one point, Kimberly sat on a rock overlooking a stream and played a hauntingly beautiful original piece. She was unaware of the hikers and tourists who stopped to listen.

They drove into the city before noon on Thursday. It had been arranged for them to meet the conductor, Dr. Andrew Morse, at his home upon arrival. Dr. Morse played violin with the city symphony and was director of the youth orchestra. When he answered the door his face lit up upon seeing Kimberly and Indiana. "This is such a pleasure," he stated as he motioned them into the living room. On the coffee table were numerous folders of sheet music. After typical small talk and inquiries about the journey he said to Kimberly, "I have a number of pieces that we are prepared to play that contain a solo for you." He handed her a number of folders, "Of course with such limited rehearsal time you'll have to tell me which you are confident you can play."

Kimberly leafed through the various folders and stated, "Any of these will do fine."

Somewhat surprised the conductor asked, "Are there any that you feel you are better prepared to play?"

"No, I've played them all and committed them to memory."

"I see." Dr. Morse took the offered music and looked through the stack. "Our orchestra is probably best prepared to play *Lark Ascending*," he pulled the sheet music, "and Brahms *Violin Concerto in D major*," he handed Kimberly the sheet music.

"We're a little light on violins," Dr. Morse said apologetically.

"When I'm not doing my solos can I play with the

orchestra?"

"We couldn't ask you to do that."

"It would be my honor. I'd love the opportunity. Please."

"Well, you could be a visiting concertmaster . . . "

"No," Kimberly interrupted, "I didn't earn that position. I'll play second violin or first violin depending on where you need me. It doesn't matter. I simply want to play with these musicians. But, I won't cause anyone to change seating. I'll take the last chair."

Dr. Morse stared at the young artist in front of him. Yes, she was young yet had an air of maturity, as well as a selfless love of music. Ego was not a factor in any sense of the word. He considered how long he had been involved in the music world and never come across such purity. How he looked forward to conducting her.

Rehearsal was to begin at six o'clock. Indiana and Kimberly arrived at five. She was too nervous to eat and had asked her father to bring her early so that she could warm up. To her relief the rehearsal was being held at a church community house performance space. When they entered, the room was empty. Indiana sat to the side and Kimberly tuned her instrument. After approximately five minutes she began playing the Brahms *Violin Concerto in D major, Op. 77*. Without sheet music she played the complex and difficult piece placing emphasis where needed and softness with a touch that was breathtaking. Indiana watched his daughter filled with pride, holding back fear, saying a silent prayer, and knowing the Black Ice Tour was a Godsend.

In a side room Dr. Morse had been preparing for rehearsal. When he heard the music he stopped what he was doing, opened the door, and listened. Technically perfect, but beyond that the emotion and expression that this child was able to convey with her interpretation of the piece was absolutely amazing. In his heart he knew he was incapable of delivering that level of performance regardless of how long he had been playing. She had talent that eclipsed all of the musicians that he had known, and yet she didn't know it or didn't acknowledge it. He listened as if it was the first time he had heard the piece and concluded it was the first time he had really heard it played in a meaningful way.

Youth orchestra musicians began to arrive. Outside the building their voices could be heard as they greeted each other and paled around. Members of the orchestra ranged in age from fourteen to seventeen meaning they were all older than Kimberly. As they entered the building and heard the music each fell silent. Quietly, they entered the rehearsal space and listened. Slowly the room filled with musicians. When Kimberly finished to her surprise she received applause. Kimberly smiled as she was surrounded by orchestra members all welcoming her and praising her playing.

When Dr. Morse entered the room the teens went to work setting up chairs. In a few short minutes they were seated and tuning up. A few late stragglers entered and were welcomed by Dr. Morse's disapproving stare. Finally, all were seated and ready to begin. Dr. Morse motioned for Kimberly to join him. "Some of you have already met Kimberly Jones. She is our guest soloist. We've chosen *Lark Ascending* and Brahms *Violin Concerto in D major.*" His assistant handed out sheet music for the two pieces. "Now, we've played both of these so you should have no problem. Kimberly is on tour and a very accomplished musician. We are very fortunate to have her join us. She has requested the opportunity to play with the orchestra when not soloing." Members of the violin section became confused and looked at each other not knowing what impact her joining them would have. They expected her to be in the first chair until she walked to the empty last chair in the first violin section.

Rehearsal went on for a long time with numerous stops for corrections by the conductor or to repeat sections that needed work. Kimberly reveled in the experience. A sixteen-year-old boy who sat to her right was constantly making humorous comments under his breath whenever they stopped. At one point Dr. Morse pointed at Kimberly when she laughed and warned, "Settle down we have work to do."

The first solo they rehearsed was *Lark Ascending*. Kimberly walked to the front. Dr. Morse asked if she was ready and she nodded. He raised his baton and the orchestra came to life. Kimberly raised her violin and began. She loved the piece and enjoyed playing it. However, this time with an orchestra behind her she had the sensation of floating, lifted by the supporting music. At the point where the full orchestra comes to life it took her breath away and she almost lost her place. Kimberly Jones entered a world she knew existed but never experienced personally. Surrounded by the mystical notes of various musical instruments she soared free. Free as the lark, free from a haunting past, free from childish concerns, free from fear, and free of a destiny that waits. Tears ran down her cheek. If she could play forever—she would. Her emotions escaped in the music that filled the room as Michail Grossman's gifted violin found its voice.

With the solo complete Kimberly returned to her seat. Silence hung in the room. The sixteen-year-old violinist beside her said, "Damn!"

After rehearsal a group of young people gathered together and discussed going out for pizza. Kimberly was with her father putting her violin in its case when one of the girls approached and invited her to join them. She looked at her father who shrugged. Off she went with her new friends.

Over pizza they talked about music and school and the upcoming summer. When they found out that Kimberly had already graduated high school one girl commented, "Are you some kind of brain or genius?"

"No," was Kimberly's response, "I just find it easy to remember things."

"Like a photographic memory?"

"Exactly." Even though Kimberly felt a little out-of-place, the fact that they were all musicians of varying talent created a common bond.

"I wish I could play like you," a fifteen-year-old girl said. She added, "I know it takes a lot of practice but when school's out that's it for the summer."

"You take lessons?" Kimberly both commented and asked.

"When we can afford it," a cellist lamented.

"We'd keep playing together if we could," another musician stated.

"When I played my solos and heard you playing with me it was as though everything expanded and the world was filled with music. It was beautiful and exciting. My notes were enhanced as they mixed with yours. It was thrilling," Kimberly stated as she looked off into the distance.

"More like trilling," the wisecracking sixteen-year-old violinist who sat next to her said causing them all to laugh. At first Kimberly was taken aback after expressing her feelings. Then seeing all the smiles she found herself smiling.

At rehearsal on Friday numerous musicians asked Kimberly for pointers, her opinion of different composers, and about the Black Ice Tour. She didn't know if they were aware of how it came to be or why she and her father were doing it. In her mind she hoped that they were ignorant of the facts. When rehearsal was over two of the older girls approached Kimberly and asked her what she planned to wear for the concert. They went on to ask, "Can I do your makeup?" and say, "I think your hair would look great up. I can help with that." It was agreed that they would meet at the college theater early.

When the concert began all of the youth orchestra musicians were onstage. The concertmaster, a young lady who was seventeen who had been accepted to a music conservatory in the fall, walked onto the stage receiving applause. She signaled the oboe player who sounded an A. The concertmaster then drew her bow across the A string and all the musicians tuned their instruments. Those steps complete Dr. Morse, the conductor, walked onto the stage drawing additional applause. After making a number of obligatory remarks he introduced their guest soloist.

Kimberly Jones walked onto the stage wearing a full length one-shoulder neckline black dress with embellished strap and embellished natural waist. The soft airy draped fabric flowed as she walked. Her long hair was up in a Grecian hair design that began with a high ponytail that was separated into one inch wide strips that were twisted and secured with hair pins. When Indiana saw his daughter his jaw literally dropped. She was twelve going on twenty-five and a vision of maturity and sophistication. That was not how she arrived at the theater.

As she approached the podium the orchestra members stood and applauded. Kimberly shook Dr. Morse's hand and turned to go to her seat in the rear. A hand grabbed her arm. The seventeen-year-old concertmaster guided Kimberly to the first chair and whispered, "We all voted and are proud to have you as a member of our orchestra." All the first violins moved one chair over.

For two nights the city was entertained by a youth orchestra that played at an amazing level and a twelve-year-old guest soloist who left many speechless. Some audience members who came on Friday night returned on Saturday.

Beyond the music, Kimberly found what might have been her first real friends. In many ways, this experience slayed a number of dragons that followed from her past. If for just two nights, she was genuinely happy. After Saturday's performance, behind the stage, the musicians chatted not wanting to leave. At one point a young girl said what many were thinking, "I wish we could play together, again."

Kimberly felt the same. She smiled and nodded and then said, "I have an idea."

CHAPTER 20

"That's a dumb idea," the seventeen-year-old concert master said after hearing Kimberly's suggestion.

"I'm sorry," Kimberly said feeling a little embarrassed.

When the older girl laughed Kimberly was somewhat confused. "No, silly—it's brilliant. I'm kidding, it's a great idea," the girl said with a broad smile. She then became serious, "I'm just afraid it's too much to set up and coordinate, not to mention pay for."

"I'm in," a fifteen-year-old cello player stated. He added, "My parents want to send me off to camp. I'll get them to donate that money to the cause."

Throughout the room different musicians made a variety of statements. "I'd like to but my parents would never go for it." "Even if I have to stowaway, I'm going." "Never gonna happen." "Do you think we can do it? That would be wonderful!" "I say we try." "This could be the best summer ever." "Let's ask Dr. Morse."

One of the musicians left the room and invited Dr. Morse and Kimberly's father to join them.

When the two adults arrived they were told of the "Kimberly Plan." As this was the last concert for the school year and the Youth Orchestra would not get back together until the fall the summer would be a silent, barren, musicless interlude that none of them wanted. Indiana and Kimberly were on tour—the Black Ice Tour. If they concentrated their schedule to do a concert every other day or every day, if the locations were close enough, over a two-week period they could play ten or more concerts. The Black Ice Tour would be enhanced by having an orchestra added, the Youth

Orchestra musicians would get plenty of playing time, and it would be an experience they would all long remember.

Dr. Morse spoke first. "It's an admirable idea, but I'm afraid there are just too many obstacles to overcome. First, there is setting up a schedule and booking concerts. Then, coordinating travel, rehearsal, and performances. Travel is a huge issue in itself. Parental consent. Not to mention the cost of such an endeavor. It just can't be done."

"Why not?" Indiana asked which surprised Dr. Morse, Kimberly, and every musician in the room. If the semi-retired truck driver had learned one important lesson from his daughter it was—nothing is impossible. Dr. Morse was correct; there were huge challenges to the plan. However, if broken down to individual pieces none were insurmountable. He continued, "If we want to do this we have to work together and tackle each element one-by-one." He turned to the conductor and asked, "Dr. Morse, if everything was to come together and the 'Summer Breeze Tour' was to happen could you commit to two weeks of your participation?"

Dr. Morse thought about a trip to New York he planned. It was something he looked forward to for some time. Unfortunately, it would be impossible to do both, logistically and financially. Yet, the opportunity to conduct a brilliant talent like Kimberly was a once-in-a-lifetime opportunity. If they did make it happen it would be a thrill for all involved including himself. He looked at Indiana and answered, "Let's give it a shot."

Cheers erupted from the members of the orchestra.

Alicia sat at her small desk in her den in stunned silence. What was in the water they were drinking? It was late when Indiana called on Saturday night. He explained that he wanted to give her plenty of notice of their plans. On the surface it was quite a challenge, however, deep inside she felt a twinge of excitement—a desire to make something memorable happen. A full orchestra was a positive factor. It was locating and booking of so many gigs in a short period of time in a concentrated geographic area that was the real challenge—not to mention cost and coordination. A smile slowly bloomed on her face. Kimberly was never short on surprises. Alicia pictured her twelve-year-old emotionally adopted daughter and wanted to reach out and hug her. In the background she heard violin music. Kimberly was thinking. Remarkably, the music was upbeat and filled with warmth and promise. Alicia didn't hear what Indiana said as her mind concentrated on that beautiful and revealing music that filled her heart with joy. Unnoticed, tears escaped from her eyes. She pushed her ear tight against the phone trying to hear every tone. A child had escaped hell, even if for a brief moment. Her Kimberly was happy!

"Do we have a concert scheduled for Thursday?" Alicia heard Indiana ask.

"Uh, yes," she answered. "Luckily, it's not far from where you are."

"Good, then Kimberly does that concert and we return here to start the 'Summer Breeze Tour,'" he stated.

"Summer Breeze Tour? Who thought of that?"

"Me. You like it?"

"What do the musicians think?"

"They didn't complain."

"I think you should let them offer their ideas."

"With all we have to do, that's your concern?"

"Sometimes, the littlest details make a big difference."

"Well, you better start getting some of the scheduling details together this week because we start the tour the week after—God willing."

"This is a little like asking me to coordinate a wedding

in a week," Alicia complained.

"It's been done."

"Yes, whose?"

"Mine."

"Oh," Alicia remembered Indiana's wife's suicide and dropped the subject. Instead, she asked, "How is this tour going to be funded? You know we share the proceeds with the non-profits but there may not be enough to support an entire orchestra."

"Sell the big blue truck," Indiana said unemotionally. Alicia was shocked, but didn't respond. She pulled up the Black Ice account on her computer to see the balance they had in the bank. The tour had proven profitable but not in the windfall sense. It would be close. "We have to make this happen," Indiana continued, "If you could see Kimberly with her new friends or hear how she felt playing with an orchestra you would understand why selling the truck is insignificant."

"Indiana," Alicia answered, "I'll make it happen on my end, but I have a condition."

"No—no, conditions."

"Yes, a condition."

With a tone of frustration Indiana asked, "What condition?"

"I want to go along."

"Go along? You going to drive all the way here? How will you coordinate the concerts?"

"I will spend this week setting up the gigs and arranging for lodging. It will actually be easier if I'm there should there be any glitches along the way. And, trust me there will be glitches." After a pause, Alicia said, "When you return from the Thursday performance you have to confirm that everything is a go. Musicians onboard, all necessary parent consent forms signed, music, transportation, funding, etc."

"Sell the blue truck."

"That may not be necessary, but I will as a last resort. Although it won't matter if you don't get all of the other steps handled," Alicia said in a businesslike tone. There was a brief pause during which Alicia heard more violin music and then she said in a very soft, caring tone, "We need to make this happen."

Chaos ensued as an enormous amount of activity began in earnest Sunday morning. Dr. Morse contacted all the parents and guardians of orchestra members by email. He asked them to sign permission forms and to contribute what they could to fund the tour. Sadly, theirs wasn't an upscale community so finances were sorely lacking, but in the end musician participation was unanimous with one exception. The seventeen-year-old concert master who had been accepted at a music conservatory had a job that she had to start. She simply needed the money.

They were able to get the loan of a school bus from the town but had to purchase insurance and were required to have a commercial driver. When Indiana told Alicia she laughed and said to him, "You're a commercial driver."

"I drive the RV—not a damn school bus," he complained.

"Calm down, Indiana, I also have a commercial license."

"You do? When did that happen?"

"Last month. See, you need me to be there."

"I guess we do."

By Wednesday a number of locations had been scheduled. Excitement was spreading but money was still an issue. Indiana called Alicia. When she answered he said, "Sell the truck."

"I like the truck."

"Sell it."

"Don't have to," Alicia stated, "Do you remember Constance Whitmore?"

"Yes, Burning Oak Farm. Of course, I remember her. She gave Kimberly Cleopatra."

"That's right, a beautiful black horse." Alicia allowed a long pause. "I called her and told her of Kimberly's plan. She said she would underwrite the entire tour, but there was a condition."

"Of course, there's always a condition."

"Stop that! This isn't a difficult condition and it saves the big blue truck."

"Oh, right. What's the condition?"

"She wants the tour to end in her town with a performance in the meeting barn. You remember that space?"

"I do. It's a beautiful area but a bit of a distance."

"I have the schedule set up to where we won't be far from there with the preceding concert."

"Great."

"There's one more condition."

"And, that would be?"

"You have to marry her."

"What!?"

"I'm kidding. However, she spoke so highly of you I think she is smitten."

"Me? No way."

"Anyway, the other condition. The girl who isn't going. She has to participate. To help, Connie will pay her whatever she was going to earn during the summer at her job so that she doesn't have to miss out."

"This keeps getting better."

"Yes, The Whitmore Tour is a reality."

Indiana ended the call and sat back to listen to Kimberly

play. So much had been accomplished in just a few days. He had to give Alicia credit. The Whitmore call was the lynchpin that made it happen. The music stopped and Kimberly walked into the small living area in the RV. Her movements were light and graceful and childlike. It was as though a burden had been removed from her that had been weighing heavy upon her restricting her. A smile reached out to Indiana. Its impact on a father's heart was dramatic. His little girl was free to be a twelve-year-old. This magic place brought her friends and expanded her world of music. If he had known what would happen this would have been the first stop on the Black Ice Tour.

"Dad," Kimberly said, "is there any way we can help Carol go on the tour? I mean, she is the concertmaster and wants to pursue music. It's just so sad that she, of all people, can't go."

"She's going," Indiana stated flatly.

With a look of surprise, Kimberly replied, "She is? How? Does she know?"

"Yes. A gift from Cleopatra. No."

"Cleopatra?" Kimberly grinned. "My horse? Mrs. Whitmore?"

"Yes, she is paying for the entire tour and the last concert will be at the barn."

"Wow! That's wonderful!"

"She is also going to pay Carol what she would have earned during the entire summer."

"That's so generous. Can I tell Carol?"

Indiana handed Kimberly the phone. She took it and danced into the rear of the RV. For a moment he stood there. How he wanted to hear the excited conversation, but decided a twelve-year-old girl deserved some privacy. He turned and left the RV. Outside it was a pleasant evening. The sky was clear and a cool breeze carried the aroma of freshly cut grass. How that brought him back to when he was a boy. It seemed so long ago. His father would yell at him for not cutting the grass. They had one of those push mowers that was a bear to use. Sweat would pour off of him and his arms would ache when he finished. It did build up his muscles. Indiana smiled. A vision of his father walking out carrying two glasses of lemonade passed through his memory.

The Whitmore Tour was ready to go. It was going to be a whirlwind event. Yet, like a whirlwind, where it was headed was not always as predicted.

CHAPTER 21

A knock on the RV door got Indiana and Kimberly's attention. When Indiana opened the door before him were Alicia and Shaun Harper wearing Tee Shirts on which was emblazoned a logo for the Black Ice/Whitmore Tour.

"You like?" Alicia asked pointing at the logo.

Before Indiana could answer Kimberly recognized the voice and ran into Alicia's arms, "Alicia! Isn't it exciting? Everyone is going. We get to play together for two whole weeks! Carol's going to do solos too. It's all coming together." Kimberly twirled in the small living area looking up.

Alicia couldn't help but grin upon seeing pure unadulterated happiness expressed by a twelve-year-old girl.

Suddenly, Kimberly stopped and got a very serious look on her face. She turned and looked at Alicia, "I'm sorry. It was you who made it happen and I didn't even say thank you."

"Just seeing you excited is all the thanks I need," Alicia responded.

"I like your tee shirt," Kimberly said as she nodded toward the shirt.

"I'm glad because we brought shirts for the entire orchestra and crew."

"Wow, we're rock stars!" Kimberly exclaimed, adding, "Can we paint the bus?"

"What?" Indiana said, "Absolutely not."

"Hey, that's not a bad idea," he heard Shaun say in the doorway. Indiana glared at his friend.

"Did you bring your watercolors and brushes?"

"No, we don't paint it—we wrap it. They do it all the time. You've seen it. It's called conformable vinyl wrapping.

A picture is printed on vinyl and then adhered to the vehicle. It can be taken off later with no damage to the vehicle," Shaun explained.

"Neat!" Kimberly said which told Indiana that it was now another element of the tour.

Indiana walked over to Shaun and said, "Since you're the expert that is your task in the next two days." He punched Shaun in the arm.

Kimberly looked at the design on Alicia's tee shirt. It depicted an abstract orchestra behind the four strings of a violin. Between the strings were the words Black Ice and below that Whitmore Tour with a black horse. She asked Alicia, "Did you design the tee shirt?"

"I did and Constance Whitmore approved it."

"I'm glad you showed an orchestra—that's important. This is their tour and I'm part of the orchestra." Kimberly smiled as belonging to the group was far more important than being a soloist.

In the afternoon there was a meeting at the church community house to finalize the details of the tour. Instead of a meeting it became a potluck celebration as everyone turned out. Long tables were filled with homemade food, paper plates, and drinks.

Kimberly sat with a number of musicians, including Carol Fontaine, the seventeen-year-old concertmaster. Across from Kimberly was Ryan Portugal the sixteen-year-old wisecracking violinist. They were all enthusiastically looking forward to the tour that was now reality. Many were interested in where Kimberly had played and were fascinated by the stories that she told. At one point, Kimberly reached for her iced tea and knocked over the glass. Cold brown liquid and ice poured over the edge of the table into Ryan Portugal's lap.

"I'm so sorry," Kimberly apologized near tears. Once again she experienced feelings of being the odd duck out. Why it had to happen at that time she didn't know. She wanted to run and hide. Damn her eyes! The tour which held so much promise dulled in the blinding light of her inadequacy. Who was she kidding? She was not a normal person who could do normal things. She was a freak that should stop trying to fit in. There was no fitting in. A part of her yearned to find her violin to express her anguish.

When Ryan stood Kimberly heard a voice say, "Hey look, Ryan peed himself." Laughter followed. Kimberly looked at the young man across from her. He returned her gaze shrugged and broke into laughter.

Carol said, "It reminds me of when Ryan knocked over his music stand during a performance. He played the rest of the piece with his chest on his knees reading the music on the floor." She laughed.

"Well, how about when you let go of your bow and it flew across the room like a spear?" he responded.

"That's right, it did. I'm glad it didn't take somebody's eye out. And, now that I think about it, you handed me your bow," Carol remembered. "Did I ever thank you for that?"

"No."

"Oh, well I better not start spoiling you now."

"Remember when Jenny coughed and her gum hit Billy in the back of the head?" Ryan said which drew more laugher. By this time, Kimberly was laughing as well. She just gave them another story to laugh about someday in the future. It seemed that she did fit in with this group of odd ducks after all.

After the meal Dr. Morse covered most of the tour details, requirements, and rules. When he finished he introduced Alicia Harper and thanked her for all the hard work she had done that went unnoticed. Alicia presented the itinerary and announced that she was the bus driver. When she finished she received a standing ovation. In addition to being overjoyed by finding Kimberly so happy Alicia found her own happiness in the satisfaction with having done something meaningful. She fully understood how Kimberly could feel like she found a home with these wonderful people.

In the afternoon most of the musicians hung around and made plans. Kimberly sat by a window and looked out. She felt drained because of all the emotions that had dragged her one way then another. At that particular moment she was content. The tour was going to be exciting and she was sharing it with people that she really liked. Her mind flashed to the end of the tour and having to say goodbye. Sadness overpowered her. Why did she have to think of that? The emotional roller-coaster continued.

A voice reached Kimberly from behind, "I think I'm mostly dry." She turned and found Ryan Portugal standing before her. He added, "It won't be the last thing spilled on this adventure. Not with this crowd of lunatics."

Kimberly smiled and said sincerely, "I'm really sorry."

"Don't be. Just know when that ice-cream cone finds its way onto your head that you owe me."

Kimberly giggled and Ryan smiled.

"You're very mature for a twelve-year-old," Ryan concluded. "I mean, you've already graduated from High School—I haven't. And, you've driven a tank, ridden in a jet fighter, and been to prison. All that I've done is live in this town, work odd jobs, and play the violin—not so well. In case you didn't notice I'm last chair."

"I think you play beautifully," Kimberly told her friend. As the words left her mouth she had a strange sensation. She wanted to encourage him but there was more. For an inexplicable reason she wanted to be with him. He made her feel good and gave her strength. There was an air of confidence surrounding him and yet also vulnerability. He was caring, kind, and good looking. And, he made her laugh.

"Don't get me wrong, I like music. I'm just not very good at it. Not like you—holy cow!"

"Thank you. Sometimes it's a blessing and sometimes . . . uh . . . I don't know."

"After this tour how long will you continue the Black Ice Tour?"

"Until dark," slipped out before Kimberly could stop herself.

"What does that mean?" a confused Ryan Portugal asked.

Reality struck Kimberly from out of nowhere. She was on a race with time and darkness was the end point. That indelible fact could not be changed. When it reared its ugly head once more it tore at her. The resulting sadness could not be camouflaged as hard as she tried.

With concern Ryan asked, "What's wrong?"

"Nothing."

"It's something. Can I help?"

"I said nothing!"

"OK, it's none of my business. I get that," he said patiently. "But, remember I'm the guy who swam up a waterfall of tea for you. Now, if that doesn't show that I care—nothing does," he smiled.

Kimberly laughed. Oh, how she ached and wanted to share her story with someone who was not a parent, doctor, or grownup. She just couldn't do it without sounding like she was complaining or in search of pity. That was the last thing she wanted.

"You know what I want to do?" Ryan changed the subject.

"What?"

"You'll laugh."

"Probably."

"See."

"OK, I'll try not to."

"I want to work on a ranch."

Kimberly laughed.

"See, I told you so. There's going to be ice cream cones coming at you from every direction. I hope you like strawberry."

"No, wait. I didn't laugh because you want to work on a ranch," Kimberly explained. "I laughed because, boy have I got a surprise for you." She thought about their last stop on the tour at Burning Oak and her thoroughbred Cleopatra.

"What surprise?"

"You're just going to have to wait," Kimberly teased.

CHAPTER 22

The Whitmore Tour was underway as an RV and school bus caravan headed east. The rising sun greeted them, promising good weather and good times. Shaun rode in the RV with Indiana while Alicia, the newly ordained commercial driver, drove the school bus. A spare tour logo tee shirt hung in the back window of the bus as it turned out to be impossible to wrap the vehicle on such short notice.

"Nice decorating job," Indiana quipped.

"I improvised," Shaun replied.

"Something tells me there will be a lot more improvising before these two weeks are over."

"And, I'm sure, a lot of surprises," Shaun remarked, then added, "In fact, I was quite surprised by how much Kimberly has changed."

"Really?"

"Indiana, you are with her every day so you don't notice. She isn't as withdrawn and I'd guess that she doesn't play the violin obsessively anymore. There's a glow around her and she has so much energy it's hard to keep up. And, I know you are keenly aware that her smile is less sarcastic and more a reflection of joy."

Indiana remarked, "She's happy—maybe, for the first time, truly happy."

"You most likely didn't notice but Alicia is also happy."

"I noticed."

"Remember when I told you I felt guilty because things seemed to always go right for me?" Shaun asked.

"Vaguely. That was like six or seven years ago, right?"

"Feels like it—doesn't it?" Shaun responded to Indiana's

joke. "Once again I feel guilty."

"How so?"

"For years I was unable to help Alicia overcome her demons until you two came along. But, you did come along in your big blue truck and my wife now has found meaning in her life, once more. In some strange way, again I catch a break. I just don't feel that I deserve the good fortune that I always receive."

"Quit feeling sorry for yourself. Did you ever think it was the other way around? That if you hadn't been such a bad driver and your pain-in-the-ass wife wasn't such a busybody Kimberly wouldn't be happy today. For whatever reasons and by whatever powers our paths crossed and we are all better off as a result."

"Our paths didn't cross—they collided," Shaun stated with a smile.

They arrived at their destination shortly after noon. After a quick lunch and checking into their rooms the members of the orchestra were given a few hours of free time before rehearsal at three o'clock. Carol and Kimberly received their request to share a room.

Kimberly sat upon her bed and examined the strings on her Michail Grossman Guarneri-style violin. Carol walked over and stood by the bed and asked, "How did you learn to play so well?"

"When I started it was so frustrating as I made just the most awful noises," Kimberly remembered. "But, then something changed. Instead of seeing the notes my mind started to hear the tones and my fingers knew where to go. To me music became a language more versatile than any spoken language on earth. When music expresses an emotion everyone experiences the feeling." She picked up the violin and played a piece in a minor key that cried of despair. Then she played allegretto which gave the impression of someone in a hurry. And finally, she played amoroso creating a picture of one in love. "If I tried to tell you about these emotions my attempt would fall pitifully short of reaching you emotionally."

"I never thought of it that way," Carol exclaimed. "I spend all my time trying to play the note perfectly."

"You play very well."

"Not like you," Carol confessed. She then said, "Sometimes I feel like a Russian ballerina."

"What?" Kimberly asked completely confused.

"Russian ballerinas do every step technically perfect but they seem sterile, without emotion. I don't want to be that type of musician."

"I have an idea," Kimberly said, "Get your violin."

After Carol tuned her violin she sat on the bed facing Kimberly.

"Now, let's have a conversation using only our violins," Kimberly suggested.

"I don't know how to do that," Carol warned.

Instead of answering Kimberly played a few tones that sounded reassuring. Reluctantly, Carol raised her violin to her shoulder and played a few notes that sounded fearful. Kimberly answered with a short march prodding her friend on. By playing the same three notes again and again, Carol told of her confusion and discomfort. Kimberly took the three notes and expanded on them creating a dance. Carol replied by playing a string of notes that steadily went higher depicting growth. Kimberly congratulated her with a flourish. A light choppy sound was Carol's laughter. In response, Kimberly played the notes from William Tell Overture, by Rossini, that depicted sunrise. Carol laughed and couldn't play anymore. She looked at Kimberly and grinned as she said, "That was unbelievable. I never thought of music that way. Wow!"

Kimberly placed her violin in its case and explained, "Music has always been how I express myself. When I'm at a loss for words I hear tones and scores in my mind. Sometimes I play and my dad gets it, sometimes not."

Carol put her violin under her chin and played a beautiful and heartfelt thank you.

At rehearsal Kimberly chose the second chair in the first violin section next to Carol. Instead of verbally asking Kimberly why she didn't take the chair of concertmaster, Carol nodded toward the chair and played a combination of notes that posed the question. Kimberly responded with music playing the string of notes Carol had played during their earlier conversation that steadily went higher depicting growth. A quick thank-you was played in response. The exchange was not missed by Dr. Morse. He found their interaction fascinating. Also, he noticed more expression in Carol's playing as brief as it was. What amazed him most was that the dramatic change had occurred so quickly. For a moment he observed Kimberly and wondered if it was due to something that she had done. He concluded that it was as the two young violinists had obviously forged a bond only they understood. As a teacher and conductor a part of him wanted to learn what inspired Carol and made such an improvement.

Different times during rehearsal when there was a lull he caught the two violinists chatting through music. It intrigued him. The universal language took on new meaning.

The performance the next night went on without a hitch. They had a reasonably good size audience given short notice and the charity was pleased. A local newspaper reporter attended the concert and gave it a glowing review.

On the third day of the tour they arrived at their next destination where they would play a concert on the following evening. Late that night Kimberly and Carol made a request. They had worked on a violin duet and asked if they could play it. At first, Dr. Morse was apprehensive. However, he had seen such talent and enthusiasm in the two girls he was inclined to allow the duet. To do so took a leap of faith because there wasn't time for him to see the piece that the violinists assured him they were ready to perform. In the end he took a deep breath and approved the addition to the program. It would be the last piece of the night.

The performance space was an outdoor venue under a large tent. A raised stage was constructed of wood while the audience sat on a hillside. The evening was warm without a cloud in the sky. More and more people streamed in as the orchestra began playing. By the second half of the concert the entire hillside was covered with appreciative attendees. Then came the duet. Each musician moved their chair and music stand to the side leaving an empty stage for Carol and Kimberly.

Two young women wearing black dresses, black tights, and black low heel shoes walked onto the stage. Both had their hair pulled back into a ponytail. They stopped in the middle of the stage and turned to face each other. Together they began stamping one of their feet. Kimberly then started playing slowly while staring at carol, then stopped. Carol played a slow response. Then abruptly they changed the tempo to that of a Celtic dance and played *Dueling Violins* by Ronan Hardiman. The quick tempo and energetic music excited the crowd who cheered. Then to the surprise of everyone the two girls began Irish step dancing while playing. The audience joined in by clapping in time with the music. On stage Carol and Kimberly smiled as they challenged each other with their music. Bows attacked strings with quick assaults, ponytails bounced with each dance step, they moved apart and then back toward each other, the music ignited the audience. Finally, they met at center stage and turned together to face the audience as they struck the final note in unison swinging their bows high above their heads. The audience spontaneously exploded with applause and cheers. When the applause continued Dr. Morse walked out and asked if they could do an encore. Upon seeing their sweaty foreheads and heavy breathing he said, "Pick it up from the last stanza." The two performers decided where to begin, walked to center stage, and did a thirty second encore that brought more applause.

Back at the hotel Dr. Morse asked, "How did you put all of that together in just a few days?"

"We didn't get much sleep," Kimberly said.

"We didn't get any sleep," Carol added.

"If you are up to it we will include it in the program, but it has to remain the final piece."

In the RV Alicia, Shaun, and Indiana sat watching a video of the performance. Alicia was the videographer and had done an excellent job. At the end of the duet Shaun said, "Just outstanding. Those two girls brought the house down. They look like they have played together for years. And, they were having the time of their lives. Something special happened on that stage." He turned from the screen and looked at Indiana and Alicia.

Two adults sat with tears running down their cheeks making no attempt to hide their emotions.

CHAPTER 23

The next stop on the Black Ice/Whitmore tour was a short distance from the previous venue. In a few hours they arrived at a retirement community made up of small condominiums. Alicia had explained that this was a free concert with no charity involved. When they arrived, the director of the facility explained that the concert would be held at six in the evening right after dinner. This posed no problem and the orchestra was on stage in the meeting house on time ready to play.

Slowly the audience entered the room. Some used walkers, others canes, but most without any aid. On this night Kimberly assumed the role of concertmaster. Once they concluded that everyone had arrived, Kimberly walked onto the stage receiving applause. The orchestra tuned up and Dr. Morse walked out onto the podium welcomed by more applause. Then it got quiet. Somewhere in the audience someone broke wind. Ryan Portugal whispered, "I think that was an e." The girl next to him hit him with her bow. It promised to be an interesting night. Just how interesting they had no idea.

The concert was enjoyed by an attentive and appreciative audience. They even clapped along during *Dueling Violins*— the final piece. With the concert over a tall man wearing a tuxedo stood and made an announcement, "We appreciate all of the wonderful talent that you shared with us this evening. We also are aware that you performed for us at no charge. Now, no artist should work for free. Therefore, we are going to reciprocate. If you would join us in the audience," he waved his arm, "there's plenty of room."

Somewhat confused the members of the orchestra left the stage and sat in the open seats in the audience. As they did they looked at each other wondering what was going on. A few of the male residents moved the chairs and music stands to the side. Then the tuxedo-wearing man took the stage. He introduced himself, "I am Holister The Great. For years I did illusions that in some cases I can't even explain how they are done." With that he took a deck of cards out of his pocket and shuffled them in the air. As he did so, one card floated out of the deck and glided down to a cello player sitting in the front row. "The Jack of Diamonds—always trying to escape." The young musician held up the card and it was the Jack of Diamonds. "Bring him home, if you don't mind," Holister The Great invited the young man onto the stage. "I'd like you to help me with this next trick," The Great said as he handed the cello player a length of rope. The magician turned his back to the audience and held his hands behind his back. "Tie my hands as tightly as you can," he instructed his musician assistant. Once tied, Holister turned to face the audience. He began to explain the trick. As he did so he said to the young man, "Move over there," and pointed with his left hand. The lad moved not realizing that Holister The Great just showed one of his tied hands. The audience laughed and Holister turned to show his hands still tied. In the end Holister The Great amazed and entertained.

With his act over, Holister introduced Ms. Suzanne Mankato while two men rolled a piano onto the stage. An elder musician wearing a long dress with her gray hair pulled back walked slowly out to enthusiastic applause and took her position at the piano. Holister The Great simply said, "*Rhapsody In Blue*" by George Gershwin." By all appearances the dexterity required to play such a piece would have long been lost but that was not the case. Fingers energized and thrilled to be where they were most comfortable forgot the aches and pains of age and danced to the rhythm of the music. Kimberly smiled hearing the expression of joy from a soul set free.

The next act was a ventriloquist with a menagerie of animals that talked, sang, told jokes, burped, and yes, passed wind. Ryan Portugal, who was sitting next to Kimberly, said, "Another e." The senior finished his act by doing a short play using shadows projected onto a bedsheet. Characters moved and jumped and fought and in the end love triumphed.

Holister The Great returned to the stage. He looked at a striking woman with aristocratic features who sat quietly by herself. She neither had to speak nor gesture to project an air of dignity and grace. Finally, he spoke, "I for one would like very much to see Natalia Marakova dance once more. When she performed it took my breath away." The woman, hearing her name, raised her head slightly but didn't respond. Holister continued, "We are all here because of the relentless unforgiving clock. But the passage of time does not drain talent it simply changes how we use it. I've seen Miss Marakova in the studio practicing when no one was around. She is as graceful and impressive as I remember. I would like to invite her to share her beauty with us and our guests."

Natalia Marakova looked around the room as if trying to decide what to do. She stood with the poise and centering of a seasoned prima ballerina and said, "One doesn't simply walk on stage and dance. Warmup is essential. I regret my pointe days are over. And, music is a factor. There is a close relationship between the dancer and the musician. Dance doesn't just happen on the spur of the moment. Thank you for your kind words, but I must decline."

From another part of the audience Kimberly stood and said, "I would love to play for you, if you would give me the honor."

"My child you may not even know the music that I require," Miss Marakova explained.

"Try me."

"Are you familiar with the solo from *Don Quixote* by Ludwig Minkus?"

"I know it." Kimberly then said, "I'm on tour trying to accumulate and save as many sights as I can. To see you dance would be a special vision I would cherish."

Natalia Marakova looked at the child across the room. There was a pure innocence that she hadn't witnessed in many years. She thought of the book *Dance Is A Contact Sport*, by Joseph H. Mazo that goes behind the scenes of a major ballet company. He adeptly revealed the long hours of practice, demanding rehearsal schedule, competition, injuries, low pay, and enormous stress faced by dancers all for the love of their art. For many years she endured the pressures of being a prima ballerina. Her mind pushed her body when it had reached its limit. She reduced calorie intake to remain the appropriate size even when weak from hunger. When injured or ill she performed lest one of her understudies supplant her and take ownership of the role. And, when the wolves were finally in the hen house she fought them off countless times until time won. Why had she pursued such a life? It was a question she didn't have to ask—for the applause. Hunger comes in many forms. With her it was recognition, adoration, and validation and she savored every moment.

Natalia considered Kimberly and thought, this child is hiding something. Artists have a sense as to the dynamics and forces affecting those around them. As a dancer she knew when her partner was not at his best before they ever stepped onto a stage. The dancer had earlier enjoyed the wonderful talent of the violinist. Now, she saw the human in turmoil. At length she said to Holister The Great, "Continue with your program the young lady and I will need time to prepare." The audience applauded in anticipation. "Come," Miss Marakova said to Kimberly as she led her from the room.

In another wing of the meeting house there was a dance studio complete with mirror wall. It was mainly used for yoga, tai chi, and other fitness programs. When they entered Natalia said, "Let me hear you play *Don Quixote* while I change."

Kimberly brought the violin up to her chin and began. Almost immediately, Natalia said from the other room, "No, no, Act 3 Kitri and Basilio's wedding celebration. That is the solo that is well known." Kimberly thought for a moment and began playing once more. "That's it. Slightly slower tempo, please, I am no longer fresh from the school de ballet." The entire piece was a minute and a half.

The prima ballerina emerged from the other room wearing a red platter style tutu with black bodice, white tights and white pointe shoes. Her gray hair was pulled back into a dancer's bun. She entered the room as a dancer would the stage gliding with every move perfection. For ten minutes she did various stretches and movements to warm up her muscles and loosen tight joints and tendons. At the end of the warmup in a no-nonsense tone she directed, "Let me mark the dance." Kimberly played and Natalia went through the steps. She made a request from time to time as to how the music should follow her movement. When they were through she explained, "At my age, it's easier for you to follow me than me follow you. Entendu." Miss Marakova walked to the starting point and produced a red fan. She snapped the fan open and instructed, "The music begins with the opening of the fan." She closed the fan and once more took her position. Kimberly waited.

Natalia Marakova stood straight and tall, shoulders back, neck extended, head tilted ever so slightly with the countenance of nobility. Standing still she was impressive. Kimberly was struck by the emotion the prima ballerina evoked without moving a muscle. The red fan snapped open and Kimberly missed her cue. Miss Marakova simply closed the fan and said, "On the fan. Again." With the opening of the fan Kimberly began playing. As she knew the music Kimberly was able to watch Natalia Marakova and adjust the music as needed. While watching the grace and beauty of the dancer Kimberly almost forgot that she was playing. Even at her advanced age the prima ballerina was magnificent. Her movement was fluid and appeared effortless. The turning of her shoulders and hips, head movement, seductive use of the fan, and unwavering pointe work projected an image of a young coquette teasing her fiancé. Natalia Marakova was in her element and she owned it.

"You were incredible," Kimberly gushed.

"It's the fan," Natalia said with a smile.

With the quick rehearsal finished Miss Marakova sat and adjusted her costume and began to put on her makeup. As she did she asked, "What do you search for, young musician?"

"What? I don't understand."

"In the large room you said that you were accumulating sights. One could interpret that as you are looking for something or about to lose something." Natalia turned from the mirror and held Kimberly's face in her hands and said, "My child, are you losing your vision?"

A cold chill ran through Kimberly as she responded, "How could you know that?" Then she added, "Did Alicia tell you?"

"You told me." Natalia returned to her makeup, "An artist performs best when she observes. Your comment and actions raised suspicion. So I observed. You favor one eye and when you come to steps you are very careful because of a loss of depth perception. And now you gather visions to recall." Marakova turned back to Kimberly, "Tonight, I dance for you. I am honored to be among your many memories. I only wish I could do *Giselle,* but it is a difficult dance even for a young dancer." She looked into the mirror, "Ah, to do *Giselle* one more time. Si seulement il pourrait être."

"Please, don't tell the others about my problem," Kimberly requested as they walked down the hall.

"My child, it is not my place to reveal such information but you realize in time it will reveal itself."

"I know, but right now I'm not the odd duck."

"You are a beautiful swan and together we are going to fly," Miss Marakova made a grand gesture with her arm and smiled.

Ahead they heard a rock band playing *Louie, Louie.* They sounded pretty good and had the room singing along.

After the "Four Geezers," what they called themselves, finished their set it was time for a little culture. Holister The Great returned to the stage. He introduced Miss Natalia Marakova prima ballerina. Kimberly stood to the side of the stage. Natalia moved gracefully to her position and struck a pose. The audience was completely silent. The red fan snapped open and Kimberly began as did Natalia. Her solo dance was better than Kimberly had seen in the studio and far too short for the audience which applauded at a feverish rate. Kimberly could see Natalia drifting back to another time and another stage and another brilliant performance. As the applause continued unabated, on a whim, Kimberly played a few notes from *Giselle.* The ballerina looked over at the violinist. Two individuals, generations apart, having only just met shared an emotional connection that gave each other strength and hope. Kimberly would face the darkness and Miss Natalia Marakova would dance one last *Giselle*.

Natalia Marakova walked to the rear of the stage and took her position. Of course, she wasn't carried to her position on the shoulders of two male dancers as she had in other performances. With arms folded across her chest and one foot back she nodded and Kimberly began. Kimberly knew the music, however had never seen the dance. The piece began slowly with graceful moves and gestures. Then Natalia did a few pirouettes on pointe and paused. As Kimberly played the prima ballerina went on pointe on one leg and while hopping on pointe on her right foot did kicks and twirls with her left. It was then that Kimberly understood why the dance was so difficult. The balance required was hard to imagine. And, the strength a dancer had to have to stay on pointe and hop eliminated all but the best. In spite of all the difficulties Natalia Marakova made it appear easy. In fact, the appearance was that she was having a good time. The dance ended with fast turns around the stage coming forward to a kneeling position front stage left. When Natalia Marakova finished the entire audience, Kimberly included, gave her a standing ovation.

Kimberly and Miss Marakova headed back to the studio. Neither spoke. Kimberly didn't know how to express how impressed she was while Natalia was exhausted from doing two solos. Natalia sat on the floor and removed her pointe shoes. Immediately, Kimberly noticed that one of her feet was bleeding. "You're hurt!" she exclaimed.

"What? Oh, a common result from dance, especially when one is out of practice. Not to worry. I will feel the real pain tomorrow from joints and muscles that have gotten too old."

"You certainly didn't look too old. It was wonderful. Thank you for the vision."

"Thank you for my final *Giselle*. If you hadn't played those notes I wouldn't have attempted it."

"Your spirit wanted it."

"I reached back in time and my heart soared. Oh, how I missed it, but now I am at peace."

Kimberly joined her friends in the main room. They were all excited by the evening's entertainment. No one wanted to leave but they had to get back on the road.

When Alicia passed she said to Kimberly, "General Humphries called. He wants to ask another favor."

Kimberly replied, "Tell him we don't work for free." She laughed and made a motion like she was snapping open a fan.

CHAPTER 24

Alicia, Shaun, Indiana, and Dr. Morse sat at a table in the dining room of the TransStar hotel. The members of the orchestra were in a back room enjoying pizza, camaraderie, and chaos. They were at the location of the next concert which would occur the following night. A large privately owned, non-profit animal shelter was the charity that was to benefit from the Black Ice/Whitmore performance. By design, they had arrived a day early so that the musicians could tour the facility.

"I spoke with General Humphries," Alicia stated.

"And, what did the dear man want, this time?" Indiana asked. He then quickly added, "I'm not flying in another helicopter!"

Alicia smiled and responded, "No helicopter." She looked at her notes and said, "He asked if Kimberly was available to perform at a VA hospital. His exact words were, 'inspiration and hope is the strongest medicine for a broken spirit.'"

"When did he request we be there?"

Before Alicia could answer Dr. Morse asked, "Where is the hospital?"

"The time of the performance is up to us. It's located a few hundred miles from Burning Oak, our final stop on this tour, yet not far from where we drop off the orchestra and return the bus."

Indiana said, "You're the manager, I just drive the RV. Can we fit it in?"

"Easily," Alicia responded, "I left time between the end of this tour and the next Black Ice concert to allow for

Kimberly to return home with the orchestra." She took a sip of tea and concluded, "She is having such a wonderful time."

Indiana looked in the direction of the back room where chaos continued. There were shouts and laughter and other unidentifiable sounds emanating from the room. Indiana thought, I don't want to know what is going on. One thing he did know was that his little girl was indeed happy. The warmth of that thought made him grateful for every individual in that room.

Dr. Morse offered, "My father was a veteran. He spent a great deal of time in VA hospitals. They can be a very lonely place." He looked at Alicia and said, "I'd like to go along, if that's possible. Maybe we could take Carol with us. She still has time before the fall semester and playing with Kimberly has made a dramatic change in her style and performance. That young lady is a wonderful teacher. I can talk with Carol's mother. Besides, the two of them would give the vets one helluva show."

"I know Kimberly would like that," Alicia stated.

"I have no problem with it," Indiana said.

"We'll have to ask Kimberly and Carol before we make any plans," Dr. Morse said as he looked in the direction of the back room.

"You going to go back there?" Indiana asked pointing at the room.

"Not unless I hear a scream and breaking dishes," Dr. Morse replied with a smile. "Besides we should ask them when they are alone."

Later in the evening Indiana and Dr. Morse sat in the RV with Kimberly and Carol. Both girls were enthusiastically in support of the idea. Immediately, they started discussing what music to play. Then unexpectedly, Kimberly said, "There is one composer whose work I have never played, but would love to."

"Who is that?" Indiana inquired.

"Andrew Morse."

A surprised Dr. Andrew Morse looked at Kimberly and asked, "How do you know about that?" After a pause he asked, "Who told you?"

Kimberly shrugged.

The next day the Black Ice/Whitmore musicians arrived at Second Chance. The facility was the brainchild of a retired veterinarian. He invested all his savings in the purchase of fifty acres and slowly transformed them into welcoming habitats for a wide range of animals that simply needed a second chance. As often as possible, pet residents were not kept in cages. In one fenced area fifteen dogs lived in peace as a pack. A pasture was home to six horses. In another fenced pen three pygmy goats, two miniature donkeys, and a pot-bellied pig shared the accommodations. Cats seemed to be wherever they wanted to be. In the main house four baby skunks had ownership of one room, while a ferret and two chipmunks lived in spacious cages. Finally, in a temperature controlled outbuilding various exotic snakes and other reptiles were housed.

As they toured, the young musicians fell in love with each critter they saw, with the exception of the snakes and reptiles. At one point they came to a small infirmary where the veterinarian cared for the many animals in his care. He explained that the goal was to ensure each pet's health and to find them good homes. There was a row of cages where animals that were being treated were kept. All were empty except one. In that single cage backed into the farthest corner was a dog. It had a black snout up to the eyes that became a mix of shades of brown. Black fir covered its back and tail while sides and legs were a mix of brown shades. Its head hung low and floppy ears framed the saddest pair of eyes in a pitiful display of despair. Kimberly stopped and looked into the cage. "He looks so sad," she said to no one in particular.

Dr. Hyatt walked up behind Kimberly and said, "She has given up. Won't eat, barely drinks, and is not responding to any attempts to bond. I'm afraid we're going to lose her."

"What happened? How did she get here?"

"We don't know much about her history. She was in a shelter, got adopted, and then abandoned. All I can guess is that she has lost hope. We tried introducing other dogs to her and she ignored them and just sits there, lost."

"That's so sad."

"She's probably a good dog, but we may never know."

"What can you do for her?"

"Very little, if she doesn't respond." Dr. Hyatt put his hand on Kimberly's shoulder and said, "We hate to see it happen, but sometimes an animal just chooses to die and we can't do anything about it." He looked at the door to the clinic and said, "We better move on."

"Can I stay here for a while?" Kimberly asked.

"I'm afraid it will only make you sad."

Kimberly forced a smile, "I won't let that happen."

"OK, but don't stay too long."

"What's her name?"

"Emma."

After Dr. Hyatt left the room Kimberly sat on the floor next to the cage. She looked at the sad animal backed into the corner and her heart ached. Even though she stared directly at the canine there was no reaction or sign of recognition in those vacant eyes. A dripping faucet was the only sound in the room.

"It's very lonely in this cage," Kimberly began. No reaction. "I've been lonely at times. Probably looked just like you. I know how much it hurts." No reaction. "Believe me, I'm the last one who can tell you not to be sad." No reaction. "But, you can have a good life. Don't throw the chance away." No reaction. "I can't leave you just sitting there." Nothing. "Please, try to understand. Don't give up." Drip, drip, drip. "You must live. Why can't you get it? Your life matters." Drip, drip, drip.

In almost a whisper Kimberly pleaded, "Emma, don't do it."

Kimberly tapped on the cage. The forlorn animal remained motionless. A desire to help morphed into frustration. Kimberly, alone sitting on a cold cement floor, felt small and powerless. What became clear was that Emma had chosen to die and nothing was going to change that outcome.

Suddenly, anger welled up in Kimberly as she rebuked, "OK, give up! Stay there with your head hung. Hang! Hang there! Leave me to feel the pain! Leave me with the guilt! Leave me more alone than anyone has ever been! Give up! But, when you did, you gave up on me when I needed all the strength there was. I stood cold and afraid and horrified and lost. If I could have joined you—I would have. How could you do it?!" Distant visions ripped away every obstruction from where emotions hide and a mournful wail escaped bringing with it a flood of tears. Kimberly cried uncontrollably. There was no stopping the flow of tears or the shallow gasps. Lightheaded, Kimberly leaned back onto the door of the cage. Tears drained her of energy. She was lost in an emotional maelstrom that gripped her tightly.

The touch of something cold and wet on the back of her neck startled Kimberly. She turned and found two brown eyes offering her comfort. Lost hope had found a reason. As they stared at each other two living creatures forgot their own pain and shared comfort with little more than a knowing gaze. Kimberly smiled, "Emma, you're beautiful." A wet tongue licked away the tears. And, a low whine sealed the alliance of two lost souls. Kimberly knew the cause of her own anguish but had no idea what her innocent friend had endured.

"You must be hungry," Kimberly said as she looked around the room. With a bowl of dogfood in hand she opened the cage door. Emma sprang out and jumped up on Kimberly. Her size and the surprise of the rapid advance caused Kimberly to stumble backward spilling dry nuggets onto the floor. "Wait. Sit," Kimberly said and the young canine obeyed. Brown eyes looked up at Kimberly and a tail slowly wagged sweeping the floor. Nuggets flew in different directions causing Kimberly to laugh. Impulsively, she hugged Emma.

When Kimberly walked out into the yard with Emma on a lead, Dr. Hyatt said, "I don't believe it."

"Believe, you'll get used to it," Indiana commented.

Dr. Hyatt walked over to the pair and asked, "How?"

"We discovered that we need each other," Kimberly answered. She then asked, "Can we adopt Emma?"

"Now, wait," Indiana started. When Kimberly looked at him and he saw her red eyes and expression he immediately knew there was far more to the story than they would ever know. He didn't finish his thought.

"Well, there's a lot more than just turning an animal over to someone," Dr. Hyatt explained. "We have to make sure it is a good match . . ." his words trailed off as he realized the ridiculousness of that statement. Emma looked at him and tilted her head as if trying to understand. "You don't have all the necessary items to provide care and you're traveling and there are fees involved and forms and who am I kidding it's the only solution." He walked over and patted Emma on the head and said softly, "You do know that she is fragile?"

"We both are."

Emma had a new home, a Ford RV. She was a quiet dog and quite obedient. During the concert she sat next to Indiana and watched Kimberly's every movement. After the performance wherever Kimberly was so was Emma. For her part, Kimberly kept track of her new friend, as well.

One more lost soul found its way onto the tour.

CHAPTER 25

There it is, Burning Oak, Kimberly said excitedly as she pointed to a metal horse statue at the entrance of the sprawling ranch. Carol rode beside her in Mozart, the Ford RV, and looked at the long white fences and large pastures and exclaimed, "Wow! I didn't know people lived like this. Not outside of books and movies."

They reached the large two-story main house and stopped in the curved driveway. Almost immediately, the front door opened and Constance Whitmore rushed out to greet them. Indiana, Kimberly, Carol, and Emma got out of the RV. Constance took Kimberly's hands and said, "Welcome back to Burning Oak. Somehow Cleopatra knows you are coming. She has been acting excitedly all day." The middle-aged woman with long blond hair wearing a casual blue dress and cowboy boots turned her attention to Carol, "You brought a friend. Welcome to Burning Oak. I'm Constance Whitmore. You can call me Connie," she offered her hand.

"Thank you so much for the tour. It has been an experience we will all remember for the rest of our lives," Carol said timidly.

"Honey, I'm the one who should thank all of you for bringing all your talent to our little neck of the woods," Connie smiled, "You can only listen to so much country music and line dance so much before you long for a little culture." Constance looked back at Kimberly and added, "Of course I do have those wonderful recordings."

"You're going to record the concert, aren't you?" Kimberly asked.

"Secretly, so you don't try to charge me extra," Connie joked.

Emma barked and wagged her tail.

"And, who is this a new member of the corps?" When she went to pat Emma on the head the canine ran behind Kimberly.

"She's still a little shy," Kimberly said. "Once she gets to know you she won't leave you alone."

Connie then turned toward Indiana who had been standing to the side, "Indiana, you look no worse for wear with all that traipsing around the country. It's so good to see you."

"Ms. Whitmore."

"I thought we got past all that formality during your last visit—it's Connie."

"Right. Connie it is good to see you. Burning Oak is as beautiful, as ever."

"And, what about its owner?"

"I, uh, you, uh,"

"Oh stop, you'll turn my head," Connie said sarcastically. She smiled having put him on the spot. His discomfort and awkwardness gave her the answer she sought. Connie pointed toward the large red barn and told Kimberly, "Cleopatra is waiting in her stall."

"Come'on Carol, I'll introduce you," Kimberly said as she hurried toward the barn. Carol and Emma followed.

"How is Kimberly doing?" Connie asked with sincere interest.

Indiana recovered from his loss of composure and smiled, "She is having the time of her life. The orchestra, the tour, her new found friends, and Emma are all dreams come true. You've done a wonderful thing."

"All I did was provide cold hard cash. The warm soft

results are your doing."

"There are times when I feel like I'm hanging onto the tail of a kite. It keeps soaring higher and higher pushed by forces unknown. I'm along for the ride but in no way the captain or the navigator."

"Don't play down your role. From my understanding you planted the original seed from which has grown an incredible series of events that have touched so many lives in positive ways. I won't say you should be proud—that's gauche—you should be satisfied with your efforts. A young woman and so many others have benefitted. Not many men can say that," Constance squeezed Indiana's hand.

In the barn Cleopatra stamped her hoof and shook her head from side to side. Kimberly patted the mare's head and said softly, "Cleopatra, I missed you."

Before rehearsal Kimberly approached Dr. Morse and stated, "I still want to play one of your compositions."

"Maybe, someday," was his response.

"No, during this concert."

"You forget who the conductor is and who decides what we play," he warned.

"Then, I won't play."

"You don't mean that."

"I don't, but if I did would you let me play one of your pieces?"

"I won't be threatened."

"Then I'll play off key."

"That's a threat."

"Oh, then I'll cough a lot."

"Another threat."

"Then . . . I've run out of threats." Kimberly smiled and then became serious, "Dr. Morse, you and the orchestra pulled me out of a dark place into the brightest sunlight I've ever known. Today, right now, I'm happy. That's something I haven't known. Simply, saying thank you is not enough. My voice is my violin. It speaks from my heart. To play something you wrote that came from your heart in some way would be something shared by us that only we understand. To give life to your music would be my gesture of gratitude."

"Kimberly, I'm not ready to have my compositions presented to a public."

"When will you be ready?"

"I really don't know."

"Then you will never be ready."

"Perhaps."

"You're starting to go bald," Kimberly unexpectedly said pointing at Dr. Morse's head.

"What?"

"Your hair is thinning. It's a flaw—you're not perfect. Are you going to wear a hat for the rest of your life to avoid criticism?"

"Miss Jones!"

"The clock is ticking—for both of us. Open the door and step out into the sunlight," she hesitated and then with a smile added, "but wear a hat you might get a sunburn."

Dr. Andrew Morse considered the young girl before him. She was insightful, unpredictable, and impetuous. With all she had endured it wasn't innocence that he saw in her. That couldn't be it. More accurately, it was an undaunted spirit. He was ashamed to admit that he didn't believe his feeble attempt at composing was worthy of being played by such a talented musician.

Kimberly, sensing that Dr. Morse might be persuaded, said, "I'm afraid of the dark. Don't be afraid of the light." She then added, "I can play the greats, but I didn't know them. I interpret notes on a paper. They aren't here to correct me or guide me. I may play the note exactly as it appears on paper but it may not be what they had in mind. You know what your music is supposed to sound like and what it is trying to convey. With your help I may for the very first time speak in the composer's voice."

"The composer's voice," Dr. Morse repeated thoughtfully. It was a unique perspective and, in this case, a winning argument. "I'll do it on one condition."

"Everybody has a condition."

"I have a chamber piece for two violins and a cello. You and Carol and, uh, Andy stay after rehearsal and we will see what it sounds like." He paused, "If we don't all agree that it is ready we don't include it in the program."

"Agreed."

Rehearsal went smoothly with everyone in good spirits and sounding great. Throughout, Dr. Morse was nervous and preoccupied with what was to follow. He had brought up the music file on his laptop and printed out each musician's part. After being in the role of teacher, conductor, and leader for so long he felt extremely vulnerable.

The three musicians set up their chairs and each looked at the music score. Dr. Morse gave them time to become familiar with their parts. Finally, he said, "Are you ready?" His brain asked him the same question. He raised his baton and the piece began. It was a combination of simple notes and runs, tempo changes, discordant tones, confusing notations, and awkward pauses. The musicians did the best they could to play together but it was unachievable. When they finished, Dr. Morse asked, "What do you think?"

The three musicians sat in silence for a moment. When Dr. Morse looked at Andrew, the boy shrugged. Then Carol said, "I, uh . . ."

Kimberly chimed in, "It's awful, not ready. I'm sorry

Dr. Morse I respect you too much to not tell you the truth."

"Thank you," Dr. Morse said with a smile. "I had to know that you will be candid with me and not pull any punches. Here is the real music."

Carol laughed and then said, "Do you know how difficult that was to play?"

"Do you know how difficult it was to write on short notice?"

Once more the musicians reviewed the music and when ready began to play. This time the room was filled with rich sweet-toned music that was elegant and refined. Without the need for words it created an image of two lovers in a quiet meadow. Then a spirited portion was introduced giving the impression of them running together hand in hand. And finally, the third part was pensive and reflective, yet filled with hope. As one might inhale the freshness of a spring day and feel renewed the music pulled the audience upward ever higher until they held the hand of God. A single violin tone drifted into heaven. Kimberly held the note slightly longer than the music score. She looked at Dr. Morse who was looking at her and she cried.

After waiting a moment, Dr. Morse asked, "That bad, huh?"

Kimberly, unable to speak, played a few notes on her violin from Dr. Morse's piece followed by a string of notes of her own. He understood.

It was agreed that the piece would be a part of the program. Kimberly recommended that it be performed just before the intermission. She told Dr. Morse, "There will be many in the audience that will want to meet you."

Indiana and Constance Whitmore road on a quiet trail together. He found that he liked her unassuming ways and direct manner. It made it easy for him to be himself. As they rode he told Connie about Kimberly's many adventures, including the terrifying helicopter ride. She, in turn, spoke of the challenges of running a large horse ranch and other business properties. Eventually, they came to a stream and decided to dismount and rest. A cool breeze found them.

"This is beautiful country," Indiana offered.

"Sometimes I come here to remind myself that there still is beauty in the world," Connie confessed. "Business can be cold and barren at times."

"You should join us on tour sometime," Indiana said impulsively. "You'd be surprised and refreshed by the good people we come to meet."

"I believe I would like that. Unfortunately, it is impossible at this time."

The breeze returned and Connie leaned into Indiana. He placed his arm around her. She drew comfort from his touch and welcomed his attention. In silence they stood looking out over the stream. One of the horses whinnied behind them. Indiana looked down at Connie, her long blond hair pulled back by the breeze to reveal deep blue eyes. She wore just enough makeup to enhance her beauty leaving her features clean and pure. Her lips were slightly parted and her expression inviting. Indiana leaned forward and they kissed. Connie turned, wrapped her arms around Indiana's neck, and they slowly lowered themselves to the ground. As if they could hear Dr. Morse's music, they became two lovers in a quiet meadow.

CHAPTER 26

As Kimberly predicted, Dr. Morse was approached by numerous audience members during intermission. Many simply wanted to tell him how much they enjoyed his piece. Others asked how he created such beautiful music, if he had more compositions, and whether or not there were recordings they could purchase. True to his nature, Dr. Morse was embarrassed and often at a loss for words. Yet, inside he was dancing and screaming with joy. The second half of the concert was equally well-received. At the end the audience was introduced to Kimberly and Carol's dueling violins and exploded with enthusiasm at its conclusion.

The next morning, over breakfast, Dr. Morse, Indiana, Constance, Alicia, and Shaun discussed the tour. They had allowed the orchestra members to sleep-in at the hotel.

"I thoroughly enjoyed your music," Connie said to Dr. Morse.

"Thank-you, Kimberly persuaded me to include it in the program."

"She does have a knack for doing that," Alicia said.

"It seems the Black Ice/Whitmore Tour has had a positive effect on yet another," Indiana concluded.

Dr. Morse nodded in agreement. He then put down his coffee cup and gave a professional opinion. "We all know that Kimberly is an exceptional musician. I am honored that she was the first to perform my composition. However, there is something else that I have noted. She is also a phenomenal teacher. The quality of play by the violin section has dramatically improved during this tour and I cannot claim any credit. A few times I caught her and the other violinists practicing before rehearsal. After seeing how well Carol was playing the others sought Kimberly out. Somehow she changed their perspective and improved their technical skills while also opening the door for better emotional expression. I've taught music for many years and freely admit that she brought out the best in me, as well."

Indiana addressed Connie, "It seems your investment has done a great deal of good. Thank-you."

"No thanks are necessary," Connie replied. After a moment she said to nobody in particular, "I'm a selfish individual." This caused the others at the table to look in disbelief. Connie continued, "I so enjoy the music that I didn't have to think twice about underwriting the tour. Now, I don't wish to let it go." She took a sip of coffee and added, "This is why I have been going over and over in my mind an idea." To Indiana she said, "Eventually all the tours will come to an end but that doesn't mean the music should cease." Indiana wasn't sure what Constance had in mind. He listened as she said, "We all know about Kimberly's condition and I believe that we should make plans now for the inevitable. If at all possible I would like to help her face her future with hope and enthusiasm and anticipation."

"At present, she is living in the moment," Indiana said, "I think it's good for her."

"I agree. However, as adults we shouldn't ignore the facts." Connie spoke to all that were present, "I have a proposal. I will donate a few acres and underwrite the construction of a music conservatory that would include a performance space, school, dormitory, and recording studio. It will give Kimberly a home and future when the tours end."

"How generous," Alicia commented.

Connie looked at Alicia and said, "As I said, I'm selfish. With all that I have I find that I feel most alive when listening to that wonderful music and being around those talented young people. In the end, I will get far more than I give."

Indiana sat silently.

Shaun stated with excitement, "I'll donate my architectural services and design the project. Of course, I'll need to do some research about acoustics."

"Kimberly would be an excellent teacher of that I am sure but a conservatory would require additional staff with a wide range of experience and talent," Dr. Morse interjected.

"Operating expenses might prove to be daunting," Alicia stated.

Connie smiled and replied, "My dear, there is a lot of money in this valley. I wouldn't even have to twist any arms or bring my revolver to get contributions."

Indiana watched the exchanges.

Alicia responded to Connie, "Of course, it would be run as a non-profit."

Dr. Morse added, "If I could be of any assistance I will be glad to help should the project become reality."

Shaun finally asked, "Indiana, you haven't said anything. What do you think?"

Indiana leaned back in his chair and simply said, "Kimberly has to choose her own direction. We can't plan her life for her."

In the early afternoon Kimberly rode Cleopatra. Next to her on a brown mare was Ryan Portugal the sixteen-year-old, last-chair violinist, who was the recipient of a spilled glass of iced tea. The two had slipped away while the other members of the orchestra swam in the pool.

"This is really beautiful country," Ryan said when they stopped at the top of a rise.

"It's the surprise that I told you about," Kimberly admitted, "I knew we would be coming here and that you would love it."

"It's quite a surprise. I do love it. I'd like to work on a ranch like this someday."

"You can. I talked with Mrs. Whitmore and she said you can have a job when you finish school."

"She did? You did? How can I thank you? I would love to work here. Look how beautiful it is."

"It's so nice here I could almost stop my gathering of . . . " Kimberly stopped herself.

"Gathering of what?" Ryan asked.

"Nothing."

"You know, every time you don't want to talk about something you say, 'nothing.' Did you ever think that I care about you? That I might want to know what is bothering you? This is the last stop on our tour. After we return home and you go off on your adventure I may never see you again."

"I know," Kimberly said sadly knowing that the reverse was probably more true—she would literally never see him again. She looked at Ryan and saw a kind face. Part of her wanted to confess about her predicament and find comfort in his arms. Yet, if he knew, everything would change. He would pity her and treat her as though she was fragile. Her burden was hers to bear.

Ryan sensed that Kimberly was not ready to share her problems, so he changed the subject, "Cleopatra is a beautiful horse."

"She thinks so."

"I like your boots," Ryan referred to Kimberly's black boots with abstract red roses inlaid and stitched on the shaft.

"Thank you. They were a gift from Mrs. Whitmore."

"She really likes you," he observed.

"I like her."

"I wish we could do something for her in gratitude for

the tour."

"That's a wonderful idea," Kimberly said cheering up.

"Why don't we get everyone together and come up with something?" Ryan smiled.

Kimberly looked at Ryan once more and tried to memorize his features. He became aware that she was staring at him but didn't say anything. Finally, he made a funny face and took her hand. It was then that Kimberly blurted out, "I'm going blind."

With a shocked expression he said, "What?"

Kimberly didn't answer. Tears welled up in her eyes.

"How? Why? When?" he stammered.

"It's already started," Kimberly said, "That's why I knocked over the tea."

"Kim, I'm sorry. Can't anything be done? That's a stupid question if something could be done you would be doing it." Ryan looked around and acknowledged, "That's why you are collecting sights."

"Don't tell the others, please."

"No, I won't." Still holding her hand Ryan said, "I don't know that you want this mug among your many visions."

Kimberly laughed through tears and replied, "It's a nice mug—one that I will keep in a special place."

"Yeah, behind the bathroom door."

"Stop, you're a good looking boy and will be a handsome man."

Ryan asked, "After the tour can we stay in touch?"

"I don't know that it's a good idea."

"I get it, sorry I asked."

"No you don't get it. When the darkness comes I don't know how I'm going to act. I'm trying to be brave, but I'm having trouble. I might become a monster—someone who people don't want to be around."

"Kim, we're friends. You don't abandon a friend because they are going through hard times. Maybe I can help. Maybe I can give you the strength to be brave."

"I'm frightened."

"You have every right to be, but you also have to know that there will be good times, and unexpected pleasures, and happiness in the future. Not having eyesight will be a challenge—that's for sure. But, even without vision you can enjoy music, smell flowers, feel the softness of Cleopatra's mane, taste pizza, listen to a good story, and hold a friend's hand." Ryan squeezed Kimberly's hand and gently held it. "If we were in a dark room we would still be together and you wouldn't have to look at my mug."

Kimberly laughed.

In the evening the orchestra met with Dr. Morse and they decided to videotape a thank-you message for Constance Whitmore. It began with a short statement from Dr. Morse followed by the orchestra playing a lead-in tune that he wrote. Then each musician took a turn and played a fifteen second impromptu solo of their own. Some were quite good and some were in need of help but the overall effect was a production that Constance Whitmore cherished.

At the end of the day Constance, Indiana, Shaun, Alicia, and Kimberly met in the library. They told Kimberly of the proposal made by Mrs. Whitmore. Indiana was careful to point out that Kimberly did not have to make any immediate decisions and it was completely up to her. When they were finished the four adults waited for Kimberly to respond. She sat motionless for a prolonged period of time. Emma pushed her nose up under her arm. Visions of the tour with the orchestra passed through her mind. How she loved all of those crazy kids. All the joy she experienced was something she would treasure. The tour ended too soon. She wasn't ready.

A music conservatory wasn't something she ever considered. In fact, she hadn't thought past the next venue where she would play. Her view of her future was a great black abyss when the tour ended. Nothing was there. No excitement, no pleasure, no hope awaited. The saving grace was music. If she could cloak herself with music she would escape an outside world that was unseen and unavailable. A world she no longer could be a part of would be a memory. She had tried to fill her mind's eye with visions on the tour in preparation. What she didn't anticipate was that she also filled her heart with unforgettable experiences and contact with an endless list of wonderful people. No longer was the world simply images. "If we were in a dark room we would still be together and you wouldn't have to look at my mug." Ryan Portugal's words reached out to her.

"We can call it Black Ice," Kimberly said with a smile as she patted Emma on the head.

CHAPTER 27

The Black Ice/Whitmore Tour was over. A tired school bus rested in the parking lot as members of the orchestra carried their belongings and instruments to waiting cars. There had been hugs and smiles and kind words shared among them. It was obvious that they were not the same group of individuals who had departed a week and a half earlier. In an intermezzo they grew, matured, lived a dream, and discovered each other. And, now they would always be the Black Ice/Whitmore Orchestra filled with pride and memories.

Ryan Portugal stood facing Kimberly. He said softly, "I won't call you but will wait for a call from you. Staying in touch has to be your decision. If it was up to me I would talk with you every day." He kissed her on the forehead.

Kimberly hugged Ryan and replied, "I can't promise because I don't know what tomorrow will bring but your mug smiles at me in my mind and brings me strength."

"Kim, we have to go," Carol called from the Ford RV.

This time the Ford RV had four occupants, Indiana, Dr. Morse, Kimberly, and Carol. Uh, five, we can't overlook Emma. It only took two and a half hours to reach the city where the veteran's hospital was located. Before entering, Dr. Morse talked with the two young musicians.

"Any hospital can be a dreary and foreboding place, but veteran's hospitals are significantly worse. The patients have either suffered severe injuries or wounds, have long-term disabilities, are ailing senior veterans, or for the most part have some other critical medical reason to be there. Overcrowding puts overwhelming demands on the staff and facilities are often past their prime. I'm telling you this so that you aren't surprised or upset. You are going to see another side of human suffering. Our job will be to bring some level of relief from the stress, uncertainty, and misery faced by these fine people who served our nation and in doing so served us.

"General Humphries picked this facility because there are a large number of young men and women who have been wounded in foreign conflicts," Indiana added. "Their injuries and situations are new to them. Some of them are soldiers that he trained. He feels that music can reach inside a man and have an emotional and inspirational impact on those who are struggling."

Dr. Morse looked at the two young women and said with a smile, "Let's talk to them as only we know how."

Chairs had been set up and spaces left for wheelchairs in the main dining hall. Carol and Kimberly began by playing the medley Kimberly had performed with Sergeant Webb at the military base what seemed a long time ago. Carol played *God Bless America* while Kimberly played *Danny Boy*. The audience response was unexpectedly enthusiastic. Each piece they played brought more applause from a sea of ailing and injured veterans who forgot their burden for a moment. The finale, *Dueling Violins,* evoked such a response that after they caught their breath the girls repeated the piece.

After the main performance, they were asked if they would visit the wards where non-ambulatory patients were located. The two girls walked through the wards playing duets. Even though their hearts were aching by what they saw they kept the music upbeat and positive. At one point without saying anything Carol began playing improvisational tunes. Kimberly joined in and they carried on a melodic conversation that proved highly entertaining. In spite of their condition veterans applauded and whistled their approval.

At one point while they walked along playing Carol whispered to Kimberly, "We could make a living at an Italian restaurant."

Kimberly laughed.

When they were through the administrator who had guided them around the facility said to Kimberly, "General Humphries made a request that you play for a young soldier who lost his sight in combat. He's having a rough time."

Kimberly agreed and was ushered through a door into a room where she saw a young black man sitting in a chair facing a wall. He appeared to be awake so she began playing her violin.

"Get out of here!"

Kimberly stopped playing. Instead of leaving she remained and stood silently in the room.

"You're still here, I can hear you breathing," the young soldier complained, "Get out."

Kimberly remained.

"Are you deaf? I don't want your music or your ass in my room."

Kimberly placed her violin on the desk in the room. She then walked closer to the patient and stood behind him.

"What's wrong with you? Don't you understand English? I don't want you here. What am I some kind of curiosity—something to be pitied? Go look at some other broken body and feel good about yourself."

Still, Kimberly remained.

Abruptly, the young man stood, turned, and swung his arm. He landed a glancing blow on Kimberly's face. More surprised than injured she cried out and fell to the floor. The man in a frustrated tone demanded, "Why don't you leave?"

Finally, Kimberly spoke as she got back on her feet,

"I'm learning."

"Learning? Learning what?"

In a low voice she answered, "How I'm going to act when I enter perpetual dark."

"What are you talking about? I'm the one in the dark. You can see."

"You're ahead of me—that's true. My descent is still to come."

"Who are you?" Sergeant Watts asked with less venom.

"My name is Kimberly and I play the violin, as you could tell."

"Are you blind?"

"Not yet."

"But, you're going blind."

"Yes."

"So, those bastards send you in here to see what it's like?"

"I think they thought that we could help each other."

"How? You gonna make me feel better about being lost in the dark by playing your fiddle?"

"It's a Guarneri-style violin," Kimberly snapped.

"That supposed to mean something?"

"It means something to me. There is an old man who gave it to me that would give up his eyesight to be able to play it once more." Kimberly thought for a moment after hearing her own words. "I will be taking it into the darkness with me. The music will light my way."

"So, why don't you take your goober-style fiddle and get the hell out of here?"

"I can't."

"Why the hell not?"

"Because you're still standing alone in the dark."

"There ya go, little girl. That about sums it up. I'm

alone in the dark. So, why don't you leave me alone?"

"Because you're lost in darkness that has nothing to do with eyesight."

"What do you know about darkness?"

"I know, I'm afraid of the dark," Kimberly admitted. "And, there are no nightlights in your head."

Sergeant Watts laughed, "You're nuts."

"I'm serious," Kimberly insisted. "I don't know that I can stand being in the dark living in constant fear."

"I'll tell you about fear," Sergeant Watts said. "At first you don't think you can take it. You want to run and hide, but you can't. Then you're not sure you can function with shaking hands. All your senses seem hyper-sensitive. The slightest thing makes you jump. Then something happens and you act before you can even think about it. In the end, you depend on fear because it can keep you alive."

"It makes my fear of the dark seem silly."

"No fear is silly," the young soldier replied, "You simply have to conquer it."

"I'm afraid that when my sun goes down that I will act like you."

"Don't count on it. Remember you have your goober-style violin and music."

"What do you have?"

"Nothing," he said sadly, "Absolutely, nothing."

The two remained silent for a few moments. Then Kimberly said in a sincere and beseeching voice, "Can you help me face the demon?"

Sergeant Watts didn't answer.

"I'm afraid and don't want to think about it. But, it sneaks into my thoughts at unexpected times," Kimberly explained. She added, "I understand your anger. I have my own. When it happens I will act as you do."

Sergeant Watts walked toward Kimberly's voice. He felt around and found a chair and motioned for her to sit. He found and sat in another chair. "How old are you?" he asked.

"Twelve, but I'll be thirteen in a few weeks."

"When I was twelve I was trying to stay out of trouble and stay out of gangs," he smiled. "They were always trying to recruit new members—mainly by scaring you into it. Join us or get your ass kicked every day. I made it into a game. Instead of them hunting me, I started hunting them. It got so I knew where they'd be and when. They thought I was a f . . . uh . . . freaking ghost. I got to where I would make them think I was going to be someplace and then I'd watch them searching that place and getting pissed off. Finally, I caught up with their leader alone one night. Snuck up right behind him, held a knife to his neck, and said I can take you all out whenever I want—lay off."

"Wow, did they leave you alone?"

"Not at first. They watched our apartment waiting for me to come out. I knew that would be the case so I never went in. I stayed across the street in an empty apartment. Then when I saw who was watching my apartment I snuck to theirs and wrote my initials real big on their door." Sergeant Watts laughed, "It spooked the shit out of them."

"Then they left you alone?"

"Now, if I did that to you, you would leave me alone, right?"

"Absolutely."

"Not these knuckleheads. What do you think they tried next?"

"I don't know. Probably looked for you at school."

"Bingo! Smart girl. They waited for me after school. But, I never came out."

"You stayed at school?"

"No, Every night the janitors would clean up and put out the garbage. I talked one of them into letting me use an old uniform and arrived and left the school with him. I walked right by one of the punks and he never recognized me." Once more Sergeant Watts smiled, "They finally gave up."

"You should write stories," Kimberly observed.

"It's kinda hard to type when you can't see the keys."

"You can dictate into a computer program and it will turn out the written document," Kimberly said. "I'd love to hear more."

"I don't think so."

"When you write you create worlds in which you can see. Did you not see your apartment and school in the story you told?"

The young warrior thought about what Kimberly said. Kimberly and Sergeant Watts then talked on and on. He told more stories and together they laughed. Finally, he asked her if she would play her violin. Kimberly explained how she creates music in her mind and told him this was his tune. It had strength mixed with tenderness, followed by powerful tones, sounds of despair, followed by a dawning of a new day. When she finished she said, "I give you a new day don't waste it."

Sergeant Watts sat in silence. In his mind he pictured a dawn and it was beautiful. He longed to breathe some fresh air and smell the flowers and trees and feel the breeze flow across his face. Kimberly's tune—no his tune—remained in his ears. It would be tough, but he would give it a try. Finally, he said, "I wish I had a copy of that music."

Kimberly replied, "I don't usually record my personal music but I did record it on my phone. If you give me your number, I'll send it to you."

"Are you sure that you are only twelve," he asked.

"Almost thirteen."

"I might try writing," Sergeant Watts said. "I probably won't be any damn good at it, but it might be fun to create some new worlds to see. You take care of yourself and that Guarneri-style violin."

They hugged and Kimberly left the room. She walked down the hall and found Dr. Morse, Carol, and her father waiting in a lounge. When she got to them she said, "I really like him and know he's going to find his way into the sunshine."

"What happened to your eye?" Carol asked.

"He punched me."

CHAPTER 28

After dropping off Carol Fontaine and Dr. Morse, Indiana and Kimberly walked back toward the Ford RV. Indiana observed, "You're limping, did you hurt yourself?"

"I must have twisted my knee during dueling violins," Kimberly replied. "It's swollen and tender."

Once in the RV Indiana examined his daughter's right knee. It was indeed swollen and when he touched the kneecap Kimberly cried out in pain. "That seems pretty bad," he said, "We should have it looked at by a doctor."

"I don't want to go down that road."

"We have to Kimberly. You're in pain and it could get worse. Don't worry, I'll be with you," Indiana reassured his daughter.

"Can we wait until we get to Burning Oak?"

"Burning Oak? What makes you think we are going back to Burning Oak?"

"Because that's where I'd like to go. Besides, Mrs. Whitmore can recommend a doctor rather than us blindly picking one out of the listings."

"It's a long drive."

"I can make it. I don't have to walk any."

After they were on the road Emma came up between the seats and pushed her nose under Kimberly's arm. She looked over at her furry companion and a wave of apprehension washed over her. With her left hand Kimberly rubbed Emma behind the ears. Big brown eyes looked up at her showing obvious concern. Kimberly whispered, "Don't worry, Emma, it will be all right." It was then that she wished she could convince herself.

On their journey Indiana and Kimberly talked about how successful the Black Ice/Whitmore Tour had been. They both avoided any discussion of what they both feared most except for the few times Indiana asked Kimberly if she was in pain. Kimberly lied and said, "No." While reminiscing about some of the events that had taken place on the tour Kimberly smiled and laughed a few times. It had been like a dream—a fantastic wonderful experience she would always treasure. At one point, during a lull in the conversation, Kimberly thought of Ryan Portugal. She wanted so much to talk with him, to hear his voice, and to gain strength from his always positive attitude. But, she also wanted to protect him from what the future might hold. In her mind, she pictured him atop his mount looking at her with those caring brown eyes and that serious expression. All he needed was the armor of a knight and the picture would be complete. She decided that if things went well she would reach out to Ryan.

They called ahead and Constance Whitmore not only recommended a general practitioner but made arrangements for her to be available when they arrived. A well-placed charitable donation wasn't required but was made regardless. Connie insisted that they stay at Burning Oak.

It was dusk when they arrived at the ranch. By that time Kimberly's knee had swollen to a point where she couldn't put weight on her right leg. Indiana locked Emma in the RV and carried Kimberly to Constance Whitmore's car. She drove them to the waiting physician.

Doctor Angela Healy greeted the father and daughter at the door and led them into an exam room. She was part of a concierge medical practice of which Constance Whitmore was a member. As a courtesy she agreed to see the child. Once in the exam room she asked the appropriate questions to determine if the condition was the result of an accident or other mishap. Kimberly told her that she didn't remember hitting anything with her knee, twisting it, or falling. It simply began hurting.

They took x-rays of Kimberly's knee which revealed a suspicious dark area. Given her past and present cancer status a complete Magnetic Resonance Imaging (MRI) scan was recommended in addition to a biopsy of tissue to be taken from her knee. Doctor Healy made arrangements for a scan the next day. To relieve pain some fluid was drained from Kimberly's knee when the tissue for examination was removed.

Back at Burning Oak the atmosphere was tense. It was a perfect example of the "elephant in the room" concept where no matter what subject was brought up all present were keenly aware of the subject that was being avoided. After dinner, Kimberly, using crutches, and Emma went upstairs leaving Indiana and Connie alone in the den.

"Indiana, I know this is weighing heavy on you and there is nothing that can lessen the stress or fear," Constance said. "I just want you to know that my home and resources are available to you throughout this ordeal."

Indiana looked at Connie and nodded. He appreciated her offer and kindness. This good-hearted woman had done so much already and now graciously offered even more. His mind was electric with nervousness jumping from one thought to another with no logical order or reason. Kimberly had endured the loss of her mother, bravely faced blindness, finally found genuine friends, touched so many people with her music, and helped so many—even a dog, and now as a reward had to face yet another demon. What God in heaven would punish an innocent child so often and with so little compassion? Anger welled up in his mind. Abruptly, he pictured an empty Ford RV that would no longer have its most valuable occupant. Before him lay a lonely dog that could not understand being abandoned once more. Dark clouds filled his world suffocating him. Once more he found himself helpless. He couldn't protect his child from oncoming suffering. He couldn't vanquish the unseen threat. All he could do was be there with her and for her and give her his strength and comfort her and offer her hope and watch her die. His mind hurled that dreadful thought at him with such force that he felt its cold pitiless slap. It was a thought he desperately wanted to avoid. Yet, it glared at him with unfeeling certainty that it was indeed very possible that the music would stop forever.

Indiana stood and turned his back to Connie. Tears streamed down his face. He tried to control his breathing as to camouflage his crying. The level of despair he felt was in direct relation to the level of elation he was feeling just a day earlier. Kim had laughed and smiled and reached new heights. And the higher she soared the greater his joy. Now, the inevitable fall was tearing at his very being.

A hand touched Indiana's shoulder. It was gentle and reassuring. He turned to see Connie standing beside him. She said in a soothing voice, "We don't know what is to come. All we know is we will do everything that we can to help Kimberly through this crisis. Hopefully, it will turn out to be minor. If the opposite is true you and I have to be her strength and her support."

From upstairs violin music broke the spell. It was pleasant and bright. Not heavy and melancholy as one would expect. Notes danced throughout the house. Flourishes were followed by long single tones. Then soft and tender emotions reached out. Indiana and Connie walked over to the couch and sat as they continued to listen. More and more melodies floated from above. A variety of tempos and sounds continued. Music from a young girl facing a new and ominous darkness seemed so bright and airy and out-of-place. It was when Indiana recognized the tune from dueling violins that he realized what was happening. He turned to Connie and said, "She is reliving the Black Ice/Whitmore Tour."

The next day they reported to the hospital for the MRI. Both Constance and Indiana made sure that the atmosphere was positive and full of hope. Kimberly saw through their act but presented an act of her own. "I wish I could take my violin into that contraption," she stated lightheartedly.

"It will be here when you finish," Indiana replied.

The procedure took forty-five minutes. It was painless and a little boring but Kimberly listened to music in her mind. At one point she saw her black horse, Cleopatra, trotting in a pasture. This image was followed by Natalia Marakova, the retired ballerina, dancing her final *Giselle*. The flirtatious confident snap of her fan made Kimberly smile. If she had a fan she would do likewise to show the demon he couldn't win. Literally out-of-the-blue she was in a jet piloted by Lieutenant O'Rourke. The scene shifted to her dedicating a musical piece to his daughter Judy. A father's love sometimes subtle, sometimes overlooked, sometimes obvious always there brought forth *Pavane for a Dead Princess* by French composer Maurice Ravel that she often played for her father. Sadly, it also brought forth the thought of her being his dead princess. She knew she had to be strong for him. What was going to happen was going to happen. It was up to her to help him face it. The duet *Danny Boy* and *God Bless America* that she played with Sergeant Vincent Webb at the military base filled her inner senses.

Clicking of the magnets of the MRI created a blues

tempo. Immediately, Kimberly heard a verse from the blues an inmate sang at the prison, "Lord I'm standin' at the crossroad, babe, I believe I'm sinkin' down."

CHAPTER 29

Results of all the medical tests took two days. During that time Kimberly and Emma wandered around Burning Oak. It was without question a beautiful and inspiring place. Life seemed to be everywhere. Birds chirped away, forest creatures scurried here and there, a breeze carried the aroma of newly blooming flowers, and soothing warmth emanating from the sun caressed a young girl. Kimberly wanted to stop time. If only she could just sit for a while and catch her breath. She wondered if other people ever had an opportunity to step off of the hyper-speed merry-go-round of life and just enjoy the moment. It was then that she decided that she would do just that—enjoy the moment. She sat on a rock next to a stream and watched the clear blue water flow past. Almost in a trance she lost herself in the flowing water. There was something clean and fresh about its endless flow. In her head she was a leaf going without complaint or concern where the water took her.

"That water comes from a spring up in the hills," a voice behind Kimberly brought her back from her reverie. She turned and saw a teenage girl with short red hair wearing a tee-shirt, jeans, and a cowboy hat sitting astride a mottled gray horse. Upon seeing Kimberly's face the girl announced, "Hey, you're Violin Girl!"

Kimberly smiled and confessed, "Yep, that's me."

"I like your music."

"Thank you."

"Are you going to do another concert?"

"No, we're just visiting Mrs. Whitmore."

"She's a cool lady."

Once more Kimberly smiled and agreed, "Yes, she is."

The girl climbed down off of her mount and said, "I'm Angela." Upon seeing the crutches she asked, "Did you walk all the way here on those?"

"I sorta lost track of time and distance."

"That happens. When I was sick I lost all track of time," she said nonchalantly.

Kimberly wasn't sure if it was any of her business to ask therefore she hesitated. Yet, the girl seemed friendly and open which made asking easier, "What was wrong with you?"

"Severe asthma—I almost died," Angela shrugged. "That's behind me now. Did you hurt yourself doing your dance?"

"No, my knee just started hurting. They're doing tests." Kimberly didn't offer any more information and quite honestly didn't want to talk or think about it. What was coming was coming and she couldn't stop it. Thinking about it only dredged up the worst images and she wanted to, as much as possible, enjoy the present day.

"Do you ride? I mean, when your knee isn't messed up."

"Yes, I have a horse that stays at Burning Oak—Cleopatra."

"The black horse?" she replied with enthusiasm. "That is one beautiful horse."

"She is and she knows it."

Angela laughed. Then in an inquisitive tone asked, "What's it like being a star, traveling to exotic places, and performing in front of big audiences?"

Kimberly thought about the prison—exotic, not really. "It's hectic and sometimes stressful but when you perform you feel alive." It was then that Kimberly wished she had her violin. She wanted to escape into her music once more. Like pulling a blanket up over her head she could find refuge from a world hell-bent on destroying her. A desire to run back into her private melodic sanctuary overwhelmed her.

"What are you thinking about?" Angela asked innocently.

"Oh, nothing."

"Not true. The look on your face shows you are worried. What are you worried about?"

"Are you always so forward?"

"It's a knack." Angela walked over and picked up one of the crutches, "You can tell me to mind my own business—people do." She looked at Kimberly and smiled.

For a brief moment Kimberly felt like she was looking into a mirror. It was not a physical resemblance, rather one of attitude and conversation style. She was, in essence, conversing with herself. "I really don't want to talk about it."

"I know, but deep down you want more than anything to talk about it. You're just not comfortable doing so."

"What makes you think you know so much?"

"Because I've been where you are."

"What does that mean?"

"Figure it out."

"Did someone send you here?"

"I came on my own—quite by chance," Angela stated. "But, sometimes chance isn't chance—is it?"

"I don't know what you mean."

"I didn't plan to ride today, didn't plan to come this way. Yet, here I am." She tried walking with the crutches. "You came all this way like this?"

"Yes."

"Your arms must be sore."

"I really haven't noticed."

Angela walked over and sat on a rock near Kimberly,

"The thing is—I'm here. What are we going to do about it?"

"Well, you could climb back on your big gray horse and ride away and leave me alone."

"Yes, I can. But then my coming here would have been pointless."

"There you go."

"I said that once."

"What?"

"There you go. I said it to my uncle who had come to see me about my breathing problem. Trust me gasping for breath is no pleasure and the last thing I wanted to do was talk."

"I get that."

"He told me that he was going to ask me to do something that I wouldn't understand but to trust him. I just wanted to be left alone," Angela nodded toward Kimberly, "like you."

"Then you know how I feel."

"Right. But my uncle handed me a glass of water and told me to drink it all. I'm suffocating and he wants to drown me." Angela tossed a pebble into the steam. "To get rid of him I drank the water. Then he held out a small container and told me its sea salt. He instructed me to take a pinch and place it on my tongue. At first, I hesitated but he insisted." She leaned forward, "Here's where it got weird. I put the salt on my tongue and after a minute my breathing seemed to become easier."

"So, are you going to tell me to drink water?" Kimberly said sarcastically.

"No, water isn't your problem—it's mine. My Uncle Dan tells me to start drinking more water, a whole lot more water. He said asthma was a sign of dehydration. I'm thinking; it's a lack of air." Angela got up walked over to her horse and retrieved two bottles of water from her saddlebag. She offered one to Kimberly.

"I knew you were going to want me to drink water," Kimberly said as she accepted the bottle.

Angela sat, once more, and continued, "Uncle Dan told me how much water to drink in a day and how much salt to take. I listened but felt that it was an odd thing to do to help breathing. I was on medication and used my inhaler on a regular basis. Exercise was nearly impossible," she looked at her horse and added, "Riding was out of the question."

"Then, the water worked?"

"Worked? After two weeks I was breathing normally. When I got any indication that an attack might be starting, I would drink a glass of water put a pinch of salt on my tongue and walla it went away."

"That's amazing. I'm happy for you."

"Amazing? It was a life-saver. I don't take any medication or use an inhaler anymore." Angela pointed at her horse, "Every time I ride Einstein," as an aside she added, "he's really not that smart, I appreciate more than you can imagine the fact that I can ride."

Kimberly smiled. Yet, it was a sad smile.

"I enjoy riding more than I ever would have if I hadn't suffered with asthma and not been able to do it," Angela concluded. "It's like those things that we have to fight to have are appreciated more. Not that I liked suffering, but suffering made everything that I'm able to do now delicious beyond belief."

Kimberly looked at Angela and noted the joy in her face and life in her eyes. She had reached her secret meadow and was enjoying the thrill of living. Kimberly envied her, but wasn't jealous. It was refreshing to see.

"So, Violin Girl."

"Kimberly."

"So, Kimberly, do you want to talk or should I go away and stop bothering you?"

The afternoon came and went and dusk crept across Burning Oak. Two young girls had shared their secrets, their feelings, and their fears. Emotions ran free. At one point Angela coughed. She immediately drank water and took some sea salt and the attack didn't occur. Kimberly drew strength from her new friend and relief from expressing her doubts and concerns. In the end, Kimberly rode behind Angela on Einstein back to Burning Oak. Emma both followed and chased the big gray horse. As Angela rode away, Kimberly realized that she didn't even get her last name.

In the morning Kimberly, Indiana, and Constance sat in the doctor's office. Kimberly wondered why they always make you sit and wait. All it does is raise the stress level. No one spoke. Doctor Angela Healy entered the office carrying a folder. Based on the expression on her face it was a heavy folder.

The doctor spoke in a learned unemotional monotone, "We have the results of the biopsy and analysis of the MRI. I've consulted with a number of specialists and oncologists and they all have the same diagnosis. It is cancer. A rare form that is very aggressive. The MRI indicated multiple locations where abnormal cells are present. Given the size of the tumor in her knee growth is rapid. Prognosis is not good. Even with extremely heavy chemotherapy we would only slightly slow the progress of the disease. It is not recommended. We can provide pain medication but no further action is advised. I'm sorry." The doctor looked up at the stunned faces staring intently at her.

Kimberly heard *Pavan for a Dead Princess* in her mind. Indiana was unable to speak.

Constance Whitmore asked the question of which no one wanted the answer, "How long are we talking about?"

"Two, maybe three, months."

CHAPTER 30

Silence hung in the car as they drove back to Burning Oak. Each individual was lost, as well as tormented, by their thoughts. Hope dashed, there was little to say. Indiana felt as though his body was alive with electricity. So much energy was passing through him he thought he would explode. His anguish brought with it anger at unseen forces that were attacking his precious daughter. She didn't deserve this or any of the other misery she had to endure. His anger turned to God. Why give life to one so beautiful if only to torture her? It just doesn't make sense and no god that would do that is worthy of respect. How cruel you must be. Then his mind turned in another direction. Take your vengeance out on me. Give me the disease from hell. Let Kimberly have a life. He knew his prayer, like so many others, would not be answered. Appropriately, it began to drizzle.

"At least I won't go blind," Kimberly said softly.

Constance turned and looked at the young girl in the back seat. Her countenance did not reveal any emotion. She simply sat motionless. What she must be feeling was impossible to know. How could one so young face what she had just been told? It brought Constance Whitmore back to when she was a thirteen-year-old. Then she was Connie Parker. She took a lot of ribbing from schoolmates because her name was close to that of Bonnie Parker of the infamous Bonnie and Clyde bank robbing couple. At the time, she felt that being a teenager wasn't easy. Now, looking at Kimberly Jones she realized that she had no idea what difficult really meant. A broken heart here, disappointment there, bad haircut, lost necklace, all the catastrophes deemed so important then seemed so silly in retrospect. Constance felt ashamed for squandering a good life. And now, even with her wealth, she was powerless to help a child she had come to feel as her own. Quickly, she turned back to the front to hide the tears.

Indiana felt that a response was necessary even though he had no idea what to say, "Kim, I, uh we . . ."

"Unlike us, a piece of maple that weathered terrible cold winters and died to produce music now will live forever," Kimberly reflected. "That's what Mr. Grossman said when he gave me his violin." With increased energy in her voice she stated, "I have to pass it on to the next deserving musician. That's what we agreed."

"We don't have to make that decision, now," Indiana said consolingly.

"Oh, but I do. Music carried me, supported me, soothed me, sheltered me, gave me life. I have to make sure the music lives on." She fell silent. Once more only the sounds of the road were heard.

Impulsively, Constance reached over and took Indiana's hand. It was an act of support that was not missed by Kimberly. She felt a degree of comfort knowing that her father would not be left alone in a big empty cold musicless world. Her father had done so much for her, sacrificed, remained strong, and made her life a wonderful adventure. Yet, he carried the burden of enormous, though undeserved, guilt. Somehow, she had to let him know how much she appreciated all he had done and how much she loved him.

"Mrs. Whitmore," Kimberly called.

"Yes."

"Are you still planning to build a music conservatory?"

"I . . . I don't know," Connie answered. "Given the circumstances, there are a lot of decisions that have to be made."

"I know you made the offer in order to give me a place to keep playing the violin when the darkness came. But, it's bigger than that. The music must live on. Black Ice needs to become reality even though I won't see it."

Constance sat for a moment having difficulty focusing. She desperately wanted to think of other options that they could try to save Kimberly. Yet, the doctors were so emphatic about there being nothing else that could be done it essentially shut down any creative thinking. The thought of a conservatory filled with music but missing the inspiration that led to its birth made it a sad place in Constance's mind. Then in a soft voice she said, "Black Ice will be built."

"Then music will live in Burning Oak," Kimberly said with a smile. "That's good. Thank you."

"Thank you for bringing such a wonderful gift to our valley."

"Dad," Kimberly said. "I need you to take care of Cleopatra and Emma. They won't understand." A cold wet nose pushed up under her arm and sad brown eyes told Kimberly that her friend knew something was wrong. It broke her heart. Emma had found a renewed life and now was once more going to be deprived of the happiness she deserved. Kimberly reached over and hugged the canine and let tears wet her coat.

When they arrived back at the house Kimberly went to her room. Indiana walked into the study and dialed his phone. He felt lightheaded and cleared his throat because he feared that he wouldn't be able to speak.

Alicia answered, "Indiana, how are you? How is Kimberly?"

Indiana had to inhale a few times before he could speak, "It . . . isn't . . . good news." His voice cracked and he started to quiver as he tried to talk.

"What did the doctors say?"

"Two . . . maybe three . . . months."

"Oh, my God. Is there anything that can be done?"

"No."

Alicia began to cry and whimper, "No, no, no, it can't be true."

Shaun took the phone and spoke, "Indiana, is there anything we can do?"

"I really don't know, Shaun. We're in shock. We don't know what to do next. I can't see through the pain. My little Kimberly. I have to be strong. How do I help her? What do I do?"

Alicia's voice came through the telephone, "We're coming there."

When Indiana concluded the call Constance entered the room. She walked over and hugged him. He fell into her arms and remained like a small boy who is afraid of thunder and lightning. Rain pelted the window and a dark gray day grew darker. Everything seemed designed to create the most depressing, dreary, hopeless atmosphere possible. Then, a violin was heard, distant and soft, it played Ralph Vaughan Williams' *Lark Ascending*. Musical notes depicted a bird ascending to heaven, breaking free from the bonds of Earth, leaving its pain behind. Both Constance and Indiana sat and listened. Beautiful tones echoed in a house filled with despair. Even at such a desperate time a child's voice in music lifted the hearts of grieving adults and brought light into the darkness. Kimberly had removed herself from her worldly burdens and found solace in music. Note after note soared higher and higher on dulcet wings. Her soul danced free without a care.

Indiana turned to Constance, "We have to assure her that music will live forever at Burning Oak."

"It will, I promise."

"I want to fill her time with visions of an unending symphony."

The music stopped.

CHAPTER 31

"You can't lose hope. Life hasn't been good to you, but it can be if you don't lose hope. I know you have the courage to face this. So, don't let me down. I'll be very disappointed in you if you give up."

Sunlight slowly crept across the floor. With it the room grew brighter.

"I can't be your strength. You have to reach deep inside to find your own. And, take that sad expression off your face. It's not doing any of us any good."

Sounds from other areas of the house and outside bespoke an awakening ranch. Activity seemed to generate everywhere.

"You know that I love you. Others love you, as well. Don't add to their pain."

A knock on the door caused Kimberly to look in that direction. From the other side she heard her father's voice, "Kim, breakfast is ready."

"Coming," she replied. Her attention returned to Emma, "He needs you."

A creature not fully understanding, sensing something it did not like, followed its only friend down to the kitchen.

Over breakfast uncomfortable small talk avoided the subject on everybody's mind. Finally, Kimberly stated, "I called Carol Fontaine and asked if there was any way she could come here. She got inquisitive so I had to tell her."

Neither Connie nor Indiana commented.

"She said she would find a way to get here." Kimberly sipped her orange juice and stated, "I've chosen her for Mr. Grossman's violin." After a pause she added, "I guess it's only right that we tell him."

"Alicia and Shaun are coming," Indiana told Kimberly.

"I'm sorry that I'm going to hurt Alicia. She has done so much for us."

"You haven't hurt her, dear," Connie corrected. "None of this is your fault."

"Fault or not, I'm the source of a lot of pain. If I weren't here there wouldn't be so many long faces, or careful comments, or avoided subjects, or hidden tears. I'm going to die—that's the truth. It would be better and easier if I would just get it over with."

"Kimberly!" Indiana interrupted, "I want you to stop that kind of thinking! Our long faces are because we care and are concerned. That kind of attitude is the absolute opposite of what would be best. I want you to think about it. If I had been given the news you were given would you feel better if I went out into the woods and shot myself?"

A surprised Kimberly, who had never seen that level of intensity in her father before, replied, "No, of course not. I'm sorry."

In a kinder tone Indiana explained, "We are all given a certain amount of time—some more than others. What we do with our time is up to us. Moments together are precious. We are here now—that's what counts."

Kimberly looked down at her plate and pushed her eggs around not really feeling hungry.

Indiana was compelled to continue. His pain would have to wait. A father's role was to be the strength others needed in times of crisis. He would cry alone in the middle of the night, but by daylight he would be the anchor that maintained stability and offered hope. It was a role he neither desired nor felt he would be adequate at. However, it was in his hands—like it or not. After winning an emotional wrestling match he said in a calm and even voice, "Kimberly, we have to start planning Black Ice."

Kimberly looked up. Tears gathered in her eyes waiting to escape. She looked at her father and wanted to run into his arms and just stay there safe from the vicious jaws-of-life. A vision of her mother hanging in the basement stabbed at her mind. He was right, that was not the answer.

"When Shaun gets here we have to give him an idea of what we want Black Ice to be," Indiana continued. "You know architects; he'll go off on some wild design if we don't hold him back."

"I really haven't thought about it," Kimberly admitted.

"The first decision we have to make," Constance Whitmore said, "is location. I have a few sites in mind. After breakfast we should visit them." She looked at Indiana and could only imagine what he was feeling and the enormous stress he was under.

By mid-day they had visited a number of potential sites for Black Ice. At that time Connie suggested that they go to a well-known local barbeque restaurant on the river. She called ahead and chatted with the owner. As a result, Emma was a welcomed guest as they dined on the covered back deck overlooking the river. The slow-moving river, tree-lined banks, chirping birds, and cool breeze made it an idyllic retreat.

"I like the hillside location," Kimberly stated.

"I'm sure Shaun will thank you for choosing that one," Indiana said. "He likes a challenge."

"If there were a row of windows facing the valley it would provide a spectacular view."

"It's my favorite, as well," Connie added.

A decision made they returned to Burning Oak to find a familiar BMW parked in front. Kimberly looked at her father and said, "This is going to be difficult."

"I'm here to help," he reassured her.

They entered the house only to come face to face with a huge stuffed elephant with its trunk raised above its head. It stood six feet tall and dominated the foyer. Emma barked and hid behind Kimberly.

"Wow!" was all Kim could say as she leaned on her crutches and gazed at the noble beast.

"In some cultures the elephant is a symbol of luck and good fortune," Alicia stated as she appeared from behind the pachyderm. "I believe Howard is going to turn our luck around and help us beat this thing." She walked over to Kimberly and hugged the young violinist.

When Indiana shook his hand Shaun said, "We had to tie the damn thing to the roof under a tarpaulin."

"I'm surprised that you got it here."

"We did get some funny looks from the state troopers."

In the den they described the location chosen for Black Ice Music Conservatory. Shaun took notes and asked a significant number of questions. After a while, Indiana suggested that they visit the site. Once there, Shaun walked around and examined the hillside. He made more notes, did rough sketches, and looked this way and that. Finally, he stopped and called the group together. When he spoke it was to Kimberly, "We can build an access road on that side that would wind around to the main building. However, rather than putting it here I would recommend that we build over there." Shaun pointed in the direction of a small stream, fed by a waterfall. There would be two identical structures on either side connected by a glass enclosed sky lobby over the stream. This way there would be the appearance of the stream running through the building. Stone would be the best façade as it would blend the structure with the surrounding landscape. All were impressed by Shaun's vision of Black Ice.

In the early evening Kimberly showed signs of being in pain but refused to take the powerful painkillers provided by Dr. Healy. She explained that she wanted to participate in the planning and decision-making as long as she could. It didn't take long to become obvious it was an ordeal that proved overwhelming. By mid-evening she accepted the white pill and within an hour Indiana carried a sleeping princess up to bed.

The next day Carol Fontaine arrived at Burning Oak. Dr. Morse provided the ride. Along with them was Ryan Portugal the last chair violinist. After Carol had explained the situation, Ryan convinced Dr. Morse that there was no way he was going to be left behind. Kimberly was seated in a chair in the den. Even with crutches, walking had become difficult for her. All smiles, the three visitors entered the room. After the initial greeting they sat.

Kimberly immediately broached the subject of the violin, "Carol, it looks like we won't be doing dueling violins anymore." She smiled, but couldn't hide a sad smile. "You know the story behind the Grossman violin. It is very valuable and wonderful to play. When I accepted it I agreed to pass it on to the most talented violinist I knew—that's you."

"I'm not the most talented," Carol confessed.

"You are, if you allow yourself to be," Kimberly countered. "Talk to them, reach them, make them feel the music. It's your key to the hearts of your audience." She patted Emma as she made her plea, "Most of all I need you to keep the music alive."

"I don't know why you didn't choose me," Ryan quipped.

Kimberly looked over at the young man who was her first crush. She knew, no matter what, he was going to keep things light and uplifting. In that way he was much like her father. Kimberly knew Ryan's positive energy might be the spark that carries her along a lonely path. She smiled and said, "I have something else in mind for you."

"Oh, what might that be?"

"When you come to work at Burning Oak I want you to take care of Cleopatra. In fact, I'm giving her to you. Be good to her."

For a moment Ryan Portugal was speechless. No joke came to mind. No self-effacing comment. No philosophical statement. What was obvious was Kimberly was making final arrangements. She was putting things in order. She was preparing to die. A cold wave of remorse flowed through his veins. It became difficult to breathe. His mind had trouble focusing. He wanted to scream. Instead, he said, "First thing I'll do is paint her brown."

Kimberly laughed, "You better not."

"This way she won't show the dirt as much," Ryan smiled but his soul cried.

Dr. Morse sat and watched the exchange among the three young friends. The Black Ice Whitmore Tour seemed so long ago. In a world so filled with endless news of the bad things people do he had the honor of leading a group of the finest individuals he had ever known. Among them Kimberly Jones was a rare and remarkable young lady. He caught himself thinking in the past tense and corrected himself. She is an unmatched musical talent and equally unmatched unique personality. What was taking place was painful to watch but it was something he was willing to endure to have had the opportunity to be a part of her music.

Kimberly pulled Dr. Morse from his thoughts when she said, "Dr. Morse I have a favor to ask of you."

"Of course, what is it?"

"When Black Ice is built I want you to run it."

The conductor, violinist, composer, teacher wanted to show humility and insist there are better more qualified candidates, but this was a once-in-a-lifetime opportunity and he wanted it. He said to Kimberly, "With your help we can make Black Ice a cradle of talent and facilitator of musical creativity."

"I don't know how much help I will be but I know it will be a wonderful place if you are involved."

Later in the day they all went to visit the site of the future Black Ice Conservatory. Kimberly remained at Burning Oak. She found it more comfortable to remain in her chair in the den. At first, Indiana didn't want to leave her alone. After convincing him that she wanted to rest and that she had her phone if she needed them he reluctantly agreed.

Kimberly sat in the den and tried to think of what else she needed to do. The pain in her knee had spread to her back and left elbow. Its intensity made it clear that she wouldn't be playing the violin any longer. Her vision in one eye was fading and she seemed to be so very tired. Fatigue and depression weighed heavy on her, dragging her into a state of semi-consciousness. Distant music called her. She found that she was ready to let go and drift among the soothing tones. Pleasing notes surrounded her and caressed her. An unexpected feeling of peace comforted her. Deeper and deeper she sank into a melodic sanctuary. The music stopped. A harsh bang savagely dragged Kimberly from her reverie. In a daze she tried to focus. Another report penetrated her mind. What was happening she wasn't sure. Once more a jarring discordant sound exploded. Clarity returned and she identified knocking on the front door.

Unsteady on crutches and in pain Kimberly made her way to the door. When she opened it before her stood a man wearing a black shirt, black pants, and a black chapeau. His eyes were a deep blue and penetrating. Kimberly looked questioningly into a stranger's weathered face.

CHAPTER 32

"Kimberly Jones."

"Yes, I'm Kimberly."

"It was not a question."

"Oh."

The man in black reached out and using his index finger and thumb held open her eye—the one in which she had lost most of the vision. He gazed into the pupil with a penetrating and probing intensity. After a few moments he stated flatly, "Ah, we don't have much time."

"Much time for what? Who are you?" Kimberly asked quite confused.

"We don't have much time," he repeated, then added, "to save your life."

Kimberly was shocked by what she heard but remained bewildered, "Who are you?"

"I'm Dan, Angela Mayan's uncle."

It took a few seconds for Kimberly to put the names together for she was not thinking all that clearly. When clarity returned she remarked, "Oh, the uncle who had Angela drink water."

"Correct," Dan entered the house. When he did he came face to trunk with the six foot tall stuffed elephant. "Ah, my friend, may I pass?" He looked over his shoulder at Kimberly and said, "An elephant with its trunk raised is said to bring good luck and fortune into a home and to have the magical power to take away troubles."

"We can sure use him," Kimberly commented as she moved slowly on her crutches.

"Yes," Dan took Kimberly's hand and led her into the

living room. When they got there he helped her sit on the couch. It was then Kimberly realized that he was carrying a black bag. For a period of time the man in black ignored her as he rummaged through his bag. Finally, he took out a number of items. The first thing he did was use a small pair of scissors to cut a lock of her hair which he placed in an envelope. He then handed her a tiny plastic cup and said, "Spit."

"What?"

"Is your hearing affected, as well?"

"No."

"Then spit."

Kimberly spit in the cup. Next he handed her a larger cup and told her he needed a sample of her urine. When Kimberly looked at him with embarrassment he simply said, "I'll wait."

After excusing herself, Kimberly went into the bathroom and following an uncomfortably long period of time returned with the half-filled cup. To her surprise Dan was holding a quart-size plastic bag filled with a clear liquid. Attached to it was a long plastic tube. He took the urine sample and placed it in his black bag. With Kimberly seated on the couch he explained, "Miss Jones, cancer is not a disease. It is a symptom of a weakness, abnormality, or abuse of some part of the body. If we can identify the weakness or injury we have a chance of eradicating the condition."

Kimberly couldn't believe her ears, "You mean I can be cured?"

"Cured? No."

As quickly as her spirits had risen they dropped with an emotional thud.

Dan rose and walked over to the window and looked out. "Come," he said as he motioned toward the yard outside.

Awkwardly, Kimberly joined Dan at the window. She peered through the glass.

"See that grass, it is healthy, is it not?"

"Yes."

"If a drought were to occur and you don't water the grass it will become weak. In those areas where the soil drains too fast or lacks nutrients the grass will die. Over time there will be numerous bare spots. It is not illness, but a lack of the necessary elements to maintain health that is the cause." He turned and looked at Kimberly, "That lawn is your body and you have a lot of bare spots. If we can identify what is needed to nourish those bare spots we have every reason to believe that the grass will regrow." His gaze returned to the lawn, "We do not cure the grass because it is not ill. We provide what it needs and it does the rest."

Kimberly stood in the window leaning on her crutches lost in thought. Hope, as small as a blade of grass, was more than she had a few minutes earlier. Could there actually be an answer? The doctors were so confident that nothing could be done. Does this strange man have some kind of super powers? Or, is he a fake? She pictured Angela atop her horse named Einstein. He helped her. How foolish Kimberly felt she had been when she said, "Well, you could climb back on your big gray horse and ride away and leave me alone." Had the girl listened all hope would have disappeared with her. Kimberly turned her attention to the man in black who stood motionless allowing her to digest what he had said. Hesitantly, she asked, "Do I have a chance to be healthy?"

"There is always a chance."

It was not exactly what she had wanted to hear—too vague and noncommittal. Yet, she wished to cling to that blade of grass of hope. A new pain located in her ankle reached all the way to her mind to dash that glimmer of encouragement. Unconsciously, she looked at the floor. A hand reached under her chin and gently pushed upward causing her to see the grass outside the window. "Your state of mind is as important as nutrition. Your body can choose to respond to therapy or fall prey to negative thinking."

"How do I avoid negative thinking when that is all there is?" a tear punctuated Kimberly's question.

"Hug an elephant," he shrugged.

Initially, Kimberly was disappointed with his response. But, then, ever so slowly, she understood his meaning and laughed with abandon. She then knew Howard, the elephant, was there for a reason. Emma, the dog, who had been curiously watching everything that was taking place, walked over to Kimberly and licked her hand. "Maybe, I should also hug a dog."

Uncle Dan looked at Emma, nodded, and said, "Sure, why not."

"What do we do now?" Kimberly asked.

Dan picked up the bag filled with clear liquid. He examined it and stated, "First, we need to slow the progress of the tumors." As if as an afterthought he asked, "Are you eighteen?"

Kimberly smiled at the question, "No, I'm twelve."

"Oh, that won't do. Are your parents here?"

"My father is out at the moment."

"I must speak with him."

"I can call him."

"Yes, call him."

The conversation did not go well. Indiana was understandably cynical and had trouble understanding what the man in black was saying. As a result, he refused to give permission for Uncle Dan to do anything. Kimberly observed the conversation and was impressed by the fact that the man in black neither got frustrated nor angry. He had a calm unruffled demeanor. When the conversation ended the man in black told Kimberly, "They are coming here."

When the four adults and two teenagers returned there were awkward introductions. Afterward, Indiana, Constance, Shaun, Alicia, Kimberly, and the man in black went into the den. Dan provided his point-of-view and explained that before he initiated an analysis of Kimberly's hair, saliva, and urine he recommended that she be given an intravenous solution of Hydrogen Peroxide, Sodium Chloride, and B12. He explained that cancer cells thrive in a low oxygen environment. In addition, he stated that it was believed that low oxygen levels in cells may be a fundamental cause of cancer. There were many causes of low oxygen in cells, among which; an overload of toxins, poor quality cell walls, lack of nutrients needed for respiration, poor circulation, and even low levels of oxygen in the air breathed. The Hydrogen Peroxide mix was not a cure, although it was hoped that it would slow the growth or spread of cancer while he did his analysis.

Indiana was still not convinced. He called Dr. Angela Healy. As it turned out he did more listening than speaking. When the call was concluded Indiana turned to Uncle Dan and said, "I'm sorry, the doctor feels your approach is unproven and is dangerous since large amounts of Hydrogen Peroxide can cause, what she called, an arterial gas embolism. She said it could cause permanent lung damage and even death." He shook his head, "I just don't think we should take the chance."

Dan continued undaunted, "Cancer cells are forming in our bodies continuously. A healthy person has an army of immune cells called macrophages that attack and engulf invaders, such as a virus, bacteria, fungus, toxin, allergen—

or a cancer cell. When the immune system is compromised cancer cell growth goes unabated." He held up the plastic bag containing the clear liquid, "This is nothing more than a means of improving the medium in which macrophages operate. Is there a danger? Anything that is invasive to the body has a degree of risk. Having a tooth filled, on very rare occasions, has led to severe injury and death. Yet, I have never had a subject experience any detrimental effect from this therapy."

"I still can't agree to it," Indiana insisted.

"I can!" Kimberly stated firmly.

Kimberly's father looked at her in surprise. She returned his gaze. He walked over to where she sat and said softly, "Sweetheart, this is not something to be taken lightly."

"I'm not taking it lightly. I think it makes sense."

"As your father, I'm going to have to be the one to make this decision."

"No, it's my decision to make."

"You're twelve-years-old," Indiana insisted, "when you're eighteen . . . " His voice trailed off wishing he could take back those words. Reality reared its ugly head and was a harsh thing to face. He changed direction, "The doctor doesn't believe it will do any good."

"As opposed to what she recommends—sit and wait to die?"

It was a cold slap that left Indiana reeling, "This . . . uh . . . stuff . . . is dangerous . . . and . . .uh . . . could kill you."

"I know, but it is at least a chance—maybe a tiny chance—but a chance."

Indiana turned to Dan, "You say it has never harmed any of your patients?"

"Never."

"But, it is not a cure, either?"

"There is no cure for cancer because it isn't a disease."

"Then what is it?"

"It is a symptom of a weakness, deficiency, or injury to the body." Dan gave Indiana and the others in the room the lawn analogy. He explained that he would do an analysis and try to identify what condition left Kimberly so vulnerable at such a young age.

Indiana softened, "Then you believe there is hope?"

"There is always hope. However, I must be honest, sometimes there are hereditary weaknesses that do not respond to treatment. Even though that could be the case it should not preclude making the attempt."

"In dog years I'm far more than eighteen," Kimberly chimed in, "I'm for taking the risk. If you think about it I have nothing to lose except a couple weeks." She rubber her knee, "And, the way things are going they won't be the best weeks in my life."

Constance Whitmore walked over to Indiana and put her hand on his arm. His attention turned to her. She said, "I will never interfere with you and your daughter. I think the rest of us should leave you alone to decide." She motioned for Alicia and Shaun to leave with her. As she turned to go she said softly to Indiana, "One question; what would you do if you were the one with the disease?"

CHAPTER 33

Indiana, Kimberly, and Dr. Dan found themselves together in the den. Dan stood holding the clear plastic bag that contained a solution of Hydrogen Peroxide, Sodium Chloride, and B12. He waited for a decision to be made.

"Dad," Kimberly said softly, "I have nothing to lose."

"I know, sweetheart," her father admitted. He took her hand and held it gently. "I've tried so hard to protect you and have failed over and over. This time it has to be your decision."

"I want to do it."

"Then that's what we will do," he turned to Dr. Dan, "You heard her."

Dan walked over to where Kimberly was seated in an armchair. He took her left arm and examined it. "There's a good vein," he observed. In a few minutes Kimberly sat with an intravenous needle in her arm.

"Am I supposed to feel something?" she asked.

"No. This therapy is meant to slow the progress of the cancer. You won't notice anything."

The next day Dr. Dan returned with his analysis results. The news was not good. In addition to various nutritional deficiencies and hormonal imbalances there was a disturbing imbalance of three key minerals; magnesium, manganese, and selenium. The first two minerals could be increased with supplements. It was the selenium that was of greatest concern.

Dr. Dan explained, "Selenium is a trace mineral, meaning we need only small amounts. This particular mineral is essential for effective functioning of the immune system, helping rid the body of dangerous free radicals that can damage our DNA, and controlling oxidative processes linked to cancer development." He ran his hand through his hair, paused, then continued, "Analysis of the young lady's urine showed selenium concentrations of 124 Nano grams per liter, which is normal. However, hair analysis, which indicates long-term levels, shows selenium to be almost non-existent. Her body is getting enough selenium in the diet but for some reason is unable to convert the mineral to selenoproteins that are used for various functions. Most likely it is a genetic defect, but years of research would be needed to determine what kind of defect."

The shock of what he heard caused Indiana's voice to sound hoarse when he asked, "A genetic defect?"

Dr. Dan continued, "You've heard of hemophilia. It is an X-linked recessive disorder that affects mainly males. The reason is that females have two X chromosomes while males have only one. For this reason the defective gene is guaranteed to manifest itself in a male while unlikely in a female. A female can carry the defective chromosome and pass it on while not having any symptoms of the disease. I tell you this because somewhere in Kimberly's genetic makeup may be a malfunctioning chromosome inhibiting the utilization of selenium. How or why it was triggered may be impossible to know."

"Then what?" Indiana asked.

"I'm afraid we've run out of time."

Kimberly sat silently listening to the conversation. There was nothing to be said. Hope was a slender thread—something one could cling to until it snapped. She rose and using her crutches made her way out of the room.

That conversation took place a year earlier. Now, Indiana stood in the same room looking out over Burning

Oak. In the distance, he saw a truck traveling up the new road that led to Black Ice Music Conservatory. Work had progressed to a point where the final furnishings were being delivered. Most likely, Shaun, Alicia, and Dr. Morse were there to direct all activities. A beautiful building that straddled a stream with soundproof practice rooms, classrooms, media rooms, a dormitory, and a performance space of which any institution would be proud insured that music would live at Burning Oak.

Constance Whitmore walked up behind Indiana and gently tapped him on the shoulder. He turned and accepted the cup of coffee she offered. The warm liquid spread throughout his body. Nothing was said as he put his arm around her. She leaned in and joined him looking out at the distant road. Construction had been done at a fever pace. It was as though Shaun and Alicia were driven by an overwhelming unseen force.

A low whine caused both Indiana and Connie to turn and acknowledge Emma an odd-looking dog with a black snout up to the eyes that became a mix of shades of brown. Black fir covered her back and tail while her sides and legs were a mix of brown shades. Floppy ears framed a pair of brown eyes that spoke volumes.

"You need to go out?" Indiana asked and Emma reacted by jumping up.

Together, Connie and Indiana walked Emma out onto the carefully manicured lawn. There was not a bare spot to be found anywhere. It was a beautiful morning. The sky was a clear blue and temperatures were comfortable with a slight breeze to keep things feeling fresh. Everything was green and full of life.

A number of horses were out in a paddock. Ryan Portugal, the last chair violinist, led another horse out to the paddock and let it go free. He had joined the staff of Burning Oak after graduating from high school as Connie had promised Kimberly.

"We need to go up to Black Ice to see the finishing touches," Connie said encouragingly.

"I know."

"Maybe, this afternoon."

"That would be fine."

They turned to go back into the house but Emma pulled at the lead and barked. Their attention focused on a lone rider on a black horse. In a trot it approached. Finally, as it drew near the rider left the path and crossed the lawn to where Indiana and Connie stood.

"I told you to stay off the lawn," Indiana said firmly.

Kimberly smiled and replied, "I forgot."

Indiana tried to show anger, but knew it was futile, "You'd better start to listen, young lady."

Connie interjected, "It's only grass. It will grow back."

"Thank you, Mrs. Jones," Kimberly said with a grin as she acknowledged their newlywed status.

"How was your ride?" Connie inquired.

"Not a pain and I saw a squirrel with my bad eye."

Kimberly was cancer free and regaining her health at a rapid pace. It happened in a dramatic manner. Two days after Dr. Dan stated that time had run out he returned early in the morning. It was five a.m. when he began banging on their door. He had not slept since leaving Burning Oak. When Indiana opened the door, Dan pushed past him and stated in a loud voice, "Where is the young lady?"

"Do you know what time it is?" Indiana asked sharply.

"Yes, time to beat this thing," the excited doctor said.

"Listen, I don't want any more false hope," Indiana cautioned. "She's been through enough."

Dr. Dan pulled Indiana into the den. Almost breathless he stated, "Autoantibodies! It's not genetic, or maybe is, but the culprit is autoantibodies. They're attacking the selenoproteins. They think they are invaders. Normally, there is no cure for autoimmune disorders. But, not this time. Not this time. Sometimes there is a trigger like a virus that sends the immune system off into a self-destructive mode. She must have been infected with a nasty virus. I found a hormonal component. Your daughter has an odd, one-of-a-kind, hormone imbalance that is most likely telling the immune system lies. It can happen to pregnant women. Now, I know she's not pregnant but these hormones are creating enzymes that send out false signals. We can fix it!"

Indiana couldn't believe his ears. He wanted to believe but too many false hopes had left him cynical. Yet, he knew they couldn't ignore any possibility no matter how slim. After one month of treatment Kimberly showed improvement. At three months, she was examined by Dr. Angela Healy who admitted that the number and size of tumors had been reduced. At first, she suggested that the initial diagnosis had been incorrect, but finally simply told them to continue whatever it was they were doing.

Dr. Dan became a fixture at Burning Oak. He worked with Kimberly, ran tests, and showed increased excitement at every improvement. Seven months after "time ran out" Kimberly was found to be cancer free. Constance Whitmore underwrote the opening of a natural health clinic run by Dr. Daniel Foster.

Black Ice Music Conservatory became a reality. Kimberly began to play again. Mr. Grossman's violin found its voice, once more. The seed of music had been planted in a sleepy valley and the spirit of a young girl shined brighter than ever.

On a table in the den was a letter inviting Kimberly Jones to play at the White House.

About The Author

Kenneth J Munkens is a storyteller with an unpredictably creative mind. There is nothing common about his work. Known for his complex stories populated with multi-dimensional characters he takes readers on an emotional and intellectual journey whose destination is unpredictable.

Enter the world that Munkens creates at your own risk. His stories will make you laugh, cry, smile, wonder, and care. Empathy serves him well as he understands the wide range of emotions involved in human relationships. His humor will sneak up on you while your heart will be stung by a depth of emotion so rare these days.

Character development is an art perfected by this author. He creates real human beings that stay with you long after you finish reading. Readers often state that they feel as though they know the characters as well as they know their friends and relatives. Many long for a sequel to continue to follow the lives of characters with whom they have become attached.

Other Works by Kenneth J Munkens:
Downtown Dreams
Rude Awakening in 1969
2076AD